LOVE AND ILLUSION

MICHAL MANKIN

Dedication

For Abigail and Lisa

CHAPTER 1

There is always a solution to every problem. You just have to find it.

CHAPTER 2

She gazed out at the distant horizon where the sun glinted on the silver water of the bay, tiny diamonds of brilliant lights sparkling and dancing across the surface of the sea. Her blond curls lifted in the slight breeze, catching the tendrils which blew across her small features. Her tanned skin was smooth and soft, just as it should be in a child of her age, many years from its inevitable coarsening, which the future would inexorably bring. Her thin cotton dress was a creamy white with flowers of red and pink linked by green fronds and twisting, trailing stems. Growing fast, the hem of last year's dress now finished way above her knees showing off her long, skinny legs browned by the constant hot sun which hammered onto the ground. Small and very petite for her six years, the other children in her class towered above her.

The land fell down in front of her in a series of low hills, valleys and dips, gradually descending to the sea beyond. Behind her, the hill rose steeply, which her mother had terraced to grow her flowers, fruit and vegetables so necessary in these days of rationing left over from the war which had finished not so many years before. The house at her back was nearly at the top of the slope and behind more garden, which held the chicken coop, terminating in the flat top ridge. This held no trees but just scrub and a worn-out path which led to the village and the smattering of shops and an apology for a bus station. She could hear their neighbour taking his geese with their excited honking for their evening constitutional along the brow of the hill as he did on a daily basis. She visualised the man walking with his long stick cut from a tree on his land with the geese spread out in a long trail behind him. He would go as far as the village, swivel on his heels, say 'home now', and the birds would about turn, fall in behind him and march home to be locked up in their pen for another day. Emily knew the routine, but the geese scared her, so she would keep well away during this ritual.

She sighed. Her eyes scanned the vista in front of her, the valley rich with trees which were not tall and towering but hung low in dull greens, having lost their brightness in the short springtime which had come and gone with such swiftness. A feeling of melancholy gripped her entire body. Does a six-year-old feel depressed? Emily could not put a name to her uncertainty nor to the lassitude and misery that she was experiencing, but it was certainly real. She looked around her at the abundance of flowers and fruit, which were her personal paradise. Tiny tomatoes weighed down dozens of plants. She and her brother Alex would stuff their mouths with the minute red rubies to see who could pack in more in one go. The cucumbers hung down from their vines and the oranges, peaches, and apricots ripened on the trees. She would walk around plucking fruit and savouring their flavour. It was her job to climb into the fig trees and pick the black and green figs from the high branches while her mother played the hose on her so the wasps and bees gathering the sweet juices did not sting her. Nothing was wrong in her life, so why this dread?

Her parents had come to live in this new country when she was just a baby, so she could not remember any other home. Her dad adored her, his youngest child, and she had the good fortune of looking just like him. He was a handsome man and knew it. He would lift her on his lap and tell her that the apple never falls far from the tree. He was so proud of her prettiness and quick brain like his own. He would sit by her bed each evening and read her a story, often one of the Hans Christian Anderson tales or something similar. She never let on that she hated these stories. They were all so frightening, with their evil witches, giants, wolves or whatever. She was sensitive, quiet, and gentle; she wanted to hear stories of happiness and satisfactory outcomes without having to feel fear en route to a joyful conclusion.

It gave him so much pleasure reading to her; how could she tell him to stop? She certainly did not want to hurt his feelings. He would also spend many hours playing repetitive board games with her, such as snakes and ladders, tried to teach her chess, unsuccessfully, and she would sit by his side for long hours while showing her how to play patience, the deck of cards spread out before them on a low table.

At the weekends, he would walk with her, hand in hand, looking for tortoises, which they would then take home, keep for a few days and then release. Scorpions were a problem and also snakes so you had to watch where you walked and never barefoot. That was the rule. Many local children would go barefoot in this hot country, but her mother absolutely forbade it and quite rightly. There was also the danger of residual barbed wire hiding in the undergrowth left over from the fighting, which could catch you unawares and rip your foot open. Emily understood the danger.

One Saturday, their local gardener was getting married in the next village over the hill, and her dad decided to take her along. He was wearing a new suit that had just arrived from London. No casual clothing in those long-gone days! He carried her on his shoulders down through the valley, avoiding big roots and treacherous livestock, but missed some barbed wire lurking unseen. He tripped, she landed hard on the ground in front of him and he also stumbled downwards and ripped his new suit on some of the jagged wire. He had some explaining to do to her mother when he arrived back home! They picked themselves up, shaken but not hurt, and carried on up the narrow track but much more carefully now, watching every step so there would be no more nasty surprises.

They arrived at the wedding finally, if somewhat bedraggled. The villagers had gathered in their hundreds for the celebration from the surrounding area; music was blasting from a group of musicians, and huge round platters filled with local delicacies and foodstuff unknown to her were being handed around. The smells of the food were tantalising, and Emily happily used her hands to stuff her mouth full of these delicious flavours. There were no knives or forks; she entered into the spirit of these local manners with great excitement. The women were dancing hand in hand while the men watched, laughing at the antics of their womenfolk. Children, from babyhood to nearly adult, darted around, in and out of the dancers wanting to join in but being told to make their own circle. The music rose and fell but soon reached a crescendo only made more deafening by the women placing their hands over their mouths and ululating.

Suddenly, in the midst of all the frenzy, dozens of men appeared bearing long rifles, which they pointed into the sky, firing volley after volley of shots into the air. People were shouting with joy at the exuberance. The noise split the air, reverberating over the hillside and into the valley, crashing back and forth like continuous thunder echoing over the landscape. Emily screamed and screamed, tears pouring down her face with terror and a fear she had never known before. Finally, her father saw her petrified body tense and rigid, grabbed her in his arms and ran down the hillside into the wadi, clutching her tight in his arms. She clutched him round his neck, desperate in her panic, almost choking him with her grip until they fell into their home and safety. It was many hours before the horror receded with much sweet talking and gentle loving from her parents.

Nursery, followed by the local primary school, passed in a dream. She learned to count, to read with ease but she could not recollect any individual moments. Daily life was a haze of nothingness, and her daily existence was a solitary one, moving round her garden, watching the plants pop up through the earth in springtime. She would run to her mother, red with excitement, to impart the news of nature once again coming up trumps. Then these tiny shoots would grow and blossom, impervious to all around them, in their tiny personal bubble. Surely a metaphor for Emily herself.

She and her brother had their coterie of friends, with whom they explored the hills and valleys, which were their personal domain. No cars blighted the quiet street, and no houses impeded their access to the deserted treasure trove just waiting to be explored. The children would run and run, Emily always lagging behind and seldom connecting, either physically or emotionally, with the other children. She tried to keep up, but she was a poor runner, always slow, but she was frightened to fall behind in case she could not find her way home. Then she would hear the bell which her mother would ring, standing on the balcony to the front of the house, which overlooked the distant bay. Its sound carried over the landscape with its compelling call back to home. Time to eat, maybe time to sleep. Freedom is a precious commodity.

Friendship is so difficult and tricky. We want it. We need it. But it often remains elusive. Emily was no different in this respect, but somehow, a close relationship remained unobtainable. The other little girls wandered around the playground, arm in arm, laughing and sharing secrets. What did they talk about? They exuded so much confidence, but Emily seemed unable to merge into the group. It was not for lack of trying, however. She seemed able to get close to one child at a time, but it was the herd mentality which was so beyond her ken. How to break the impenetrable field force, which was like a metal railing surrounding the group of giggling girls? She stood to one side and watched them, observing how they inter-connected but totally incapable of joining in. She felt alone and lonely, shy and sad. She was highly intelligent, serious and thoughtful. It was the inanity of the giggling conversations that was beyond her. The pointless jumble of words which said nothing and were meaningless, in an endless stream. Standing on the hillside, she sighed again and appreciated that it was her loneliness that bore her down. Her friends stood apart from her. A close connection was somehow missing, and she did not know how to overcome this problem.

Emily was a daddy's girl. Her older brother was the delight and pride of her mother. She was bewildered by this. Basking in her father's devotion, nevertheless, the total lack of contact, both physical and emotional, between mother and daughter, was hurtful and destructive. Her brother was neither her friend nor protector. He was sly, always ready to put the blame on her when he had done something wrong. She never spoke up when this happened, keeping silent each and every time but nevertheless upset and resentful. This was to underwrite her attitude in life, which would come back to haunt her – the fear of putting her displeasure into words which could be heard in order to protect herself. It was to destroy her self-confidence and sense of her emotional balance. On the odd occasion when she had protested her innocence, she would be ignored and accused of misrepresenting the truth, and so she turned inward. Her silence became part and parcel of her very essence, which would destroy her life. Emily was never punished. It was more insidious. Never in her life would she be smacked by her parents, chastised or sent to her room. No-one shouted. There was no violence or menace. The punishment for Emily was the disbelief and sense of disappointment her mother felt in her behaviour. The fallout was the destruction of her naturally outgoing personality, which was fatally stunted and eventually annihilated.

Generally, however, life was idyllic. She was surrounded by beauty in all directions and as far as the eye could see. Wild flowers grew profusely. There were multi-coloured anemones with their vibrant reds, purples and blues. The cyclamens were everywhere, peeping out of every crevice. Jacaranda trees with their bright spring flowers and the delight of the oleander shrubs in pink and white, which lined the streets in the village and on the hillsides. Emily was happiest sitting on the dirt ground with a drawing pad and pencils, trying to put all this abundance onto paper. Not for her dolls and tea parties, for which she just could not understand the attraction. When some foolhardy person gave her a present of an exquisite and very expensive doll brought from abroad, she saw the look of horror on her mother's face who realised what was about to happen. Emily politely thanked the visitor who had come all the way from America with this treasure for her, took the doll into the garden, and assessed how it could be improved. She immediately restyled the hair with a big pair of scissors and stripped it of its clothes in order to see how they were constructed. Having achieved her aim of discovering its secrets, she then abandoned the doll, never to look at it again. No, dolls and Emily definitely did not make good playmates.

She was given pocket money each week to do, as she pleased. The village was small but with a few essential shops in its heart. She would meander down to the centre, clutching her small amount of coins to wander round to decide how to spend it. The choice was limited. Rationing still was severe so sweets were out of the question except on special occasions. She would have no option but to let the small sums mount up, and so she bought books at a small kiosk, which also sold so many other bits and bobs. Her very first was an edition of Dr Doolittle with big, brightly coloured illustrations. The cover was a heavy card with a menagerie of tropical animals and flora in brilliant colours. She read it repeatedly, and it was her first treasure. In time, it disappeared from her shelves in one of her many clear outs. She did so hate clutter.

Freedom to roam without fear was one of the many benefits of living in a small community where everyone knew each other, cars in the streets were rare, and children could run around the streets and hills without concern. Parents would just stand outside to summon their children home and someone would respond. Hardly anyone had a phone, and no-one had any apprehension for their children's welfare. As a result, the kids grew up slim, healthy and without anxiety. If hunger became an issue, the hillsides were a smorgasbord of fruit trees and wild vegetables, ready for the picking. Emily was no different. It never crossed her mind that she could be at risk and this lack of trepidation was totally justified. Little time was spent indoors when the big outside beckoned so beguilingly. Hands-off parenting was the norm.

Occasionally, the excitement of the day would be a trip to the local big town, which was about twenty minutes away by bus and where Emily's father had his business. This ramshackle transportation lacked all human comforts; seats were wooden with no upholstery and there was certainly no air-conditioning. The journey was all downhill, along steep, winding, narrow roads, and there would be a mad dash to grab seats on the shady side. The alternative was to broil in the intense heat pounding through the windows. The bus would be filled to overflowing with humans, chickens, ducks and the occasional goat being taken to the city to be sold. Often, a chicken's feather would fly up your nose and make you sneeze. On arrival, you would try to get up off your seat, but your backside would be firmly stuck because of the sweating, and eventually, with a loud sucking noise, you would manage to detach yourself. But never mind, the strong sunlight would very quickly dry your sodden skirt.

Then, mother and daughter would meander down the crowded, narrow streets, gazing at the produce on offer. There were huge barrels filled with different coloured olives, pickled cucumbers and other vegetables. Wonderful soused herrings abounded. Then, there were yet more barrels filled with dry goods, beans, lentils and rice. Big bowls of fabulous coloured spices such as turmeric, curry and paprika were truly a feast for the eyes and the senses. Emily adored it all.

Life continued in its mundane routine. School was six days a week, but home by lunchtime. Then, the afternoons were spent surveying her precious garden to assess what had sprung up and what was not thriving. As soon as she caught sight of a new shoot poking through the dry earth, she would give it a mental marker so she could keep an eye on its progress. Mother and daughter would then gaze down at this new potential treasure with huge delight at the promise to come. The fruit trees were heavy with their produce, and she would pluck the sweet loveliness and fill her mouth with their juices. For some reason, totally unfounded, Emily held a fear that she was not actually allowed to pick the fruit without permission. There was no basis for this thought, but consequently, she assumed that she had to hide the evidence from her parents. What to do with the tell-tale pips and stones? The answer was to swallow them! Many years later, when she told people what she had done over such a long period, the look of horror on their faces was quite something to behold. Emily would also laugh inwardly when people made such a fuss about removing the pips from grapes before popping them into their mouths. After all, she had never come to any harm.

There were also the chickens to look after. They lived in their large pen made out of wiring at the rear of the garden. They were the consequence of the shortages caused by the rationing and were to provide a regular supply of eggs and protein. Emily would go out each morning to search for the eggs and knew all the hiding places where they could be found. Her mother was in overall charge of the chickens' welfare and Emily was the mere assistant. For a short period, her mother also decided to keep turkeys, but it turned out she was terrified of them. They landed up in the oven, roasted to perfection, to be served with gravy, potatoes and vegetables fresh from the garden.

Living in the countryside on the side of a hill also resulted in the animal kingdom being a constant reminder that we humans are intruders. Wild cats abounded, breeding rapidly and living short, difficult, hungry lives. Fridges were still a luxury, but Emily's parents had a gleaming model in the corner of the kitchen, so they were not reliant on the huge blocks of ice brought round by a man with a mule plus trailer. The back of the fridge was not enclosed totally to protect the engine, and one day, a kitten ventured in from the garden through the open door and explored this noisy contraption. He was caught up in the mechanism and died a miserable death. His explorations also destroyed the fridge and a new model had to be ordered from America, which was bigger and even shinier.

Emily's mother was not a brave adventurer when it came to wildlife. One day, she found a couple of snakes on the back terrace close to the back door. She screamed and panicked, grabbed her two small children and dragged them into the house, bolting the door behind them. Did she think the snakes could turn the knob? She then shouted to the neighbour's gardener to come and rescue her. It turned out the snakes were harmless and the family survived to tell the story.

Emily would regularly walk to the village with her mother to do the shopping necessary. Fish was sold live as refrigeration was not widely available. There were large tanks with the fish swimming around lazily, and her mother would choose which was suitable for dinner that evening. Being British, however, she would demand that the fishmonger kill them first before wrapping them in newspaper and handing them over. On the walk home over the brow of the hill, Emily noticed that the paper packaging seemed to be moving. She gleefully pointed this fact out. Her mother yelped and raced home with Emily panting behind her. Once safely indoors, her mother ran water into the bath and dropped the very live fish in. They swam around happily for a few hours of reprieve until her father came home from work and despatched the fish into the next world, ready to be gutted and cooked and served up on a platter.

These happy interludes punctuated the routine of the days spent in hot, burning sunshine. Rain was infrequent and seasonal and when it came, it was torrential. There would be hailstones large as golf balls and storms with mammoth crashing, thunder, and lightning, which lasted for hours but with no rain whatsoever. This did not frighten Emily. On the contrary, she would listen to the cacophony, safe and protected in her dry home within the safe arms of her parents.

CHAPTER 3

There were many serious conversations round the table between her parents. Emily could not understand them at all. There was talk of money, lifestyle, disappointment. It sounded important and worrying. Your parents should not have such issues. There would be sudden silences when they realised that she was listening closely, and the talk would continue late into the night when Emily had been sent to bed. She could hear the rise and fall of their voices from the balcony on which they spent the cooler evenings overlooking the valley. She could not make out the words, and she would fall asleep to the lull of their voices which soothed her after a day of activity and learning and running around the valleys below.

The day came when her mother and father sat her and her brother down and told them that they were leaving this paradise and returning to live in England. Emily knew all about England. They regularly went on holiday there for long periods during the summer so that her fair-skinned mother could escape the stifling temperature, which was inescapable. No air-conditioning cooled the houses in those days, and her mother suffered badly from the unremitting heat. Now, their return would be permanent.

Her father disappeared first to pave the way for his family to follow. He would set up a new business, find a home and prepare the way for them to come. It was a long process and would not be easy. Her dad was a middle-aged man with a fully-fledged family, and he would have to start again from scratch. The politics of their old life meant they could not take their money and possessions with them. All that would have to stay behind. He was a grafter and a clever man, a good businessman but it all takes time. He was gone for several months.

One day, the moment arrived, and Emily and her brother accompanied their mother to the airport to catch the long flight to London. No jet planes in those days, just a propeller plane. Emily knew the drill. The engines would start and the propellers would roar. Her mother would sit beside her, clutching a pile of brown paper bags, which Emily would fill with her vomit throughout the entire flight! The flight attendant would bring her sweets and crayons to keep her mind off what was happening, but the best part of the journey was definitely the landing.

They had left the heat and sunshine behind. It was late at night on the last day of August, and it was raining.

The taxi wound its way through the dark, wet streets into London and its suburbs and down the high road with its shuttered shops, which led them to Hampstead, where her dad had rented a flat for them. There was a zebra crossing on the corner of what was to be their new street and the raindrops glistened in the flashing yellow lights of the Belisha beacons and bounced off the tarmac. It was a thing of beauty, thought Emily. She found it magical.

The flat was ghastly. Emily wandered round, checking out every aspect of this dreary new home. The inspection did not take long. It had two bedrooms, a kitchen the size of a broom cupboard as an adjunct of the roomy, high-ceilinged living room and a bathroom which echoed and was ridiculously huge. It was painted brown everywhere. Brown linoleum covered the floors, and brown-painted walls with brown paintwork to provide variety. It was certainly a far cry from their beautiful home on the hilltop, airy and filled with light and surrounded by a large, fabulous tropical garden.

It had taken her father months to find it. Landlords put up signs on the 'To Let' notices. No blacks, no Irish, no children. Discrimination was rife, and no laws existed to censor or prevent it. Nevertheless, the flat was close to transport, schools and the shops. There was no phone, just a red public phone box at the corner outside the police station. Another advantage was that a very famous violinist lived in the house directly opposite and her mother would throw open the window to listen to him practising. The flat would also be very temporary, and they just had to survive the freezing winter with inadequate heating. For Emily, it was the start of many years of suffering from red, swollen chilblains, which caused her agony through the icy months. There was no money for fur-lined boots, only Wellington boots, which offered little protection. Ironically, in future years, this miserable flat, refurbished and upgraded, would be worth a fortune for being in the heart of trendy Hampstead.

She loved life in London and did not miss her old life at all. This was very strange. They had left behind a wonderful climate, a gorgeous garden and a beautiful home. London was cold, wet and miserable. The flat was horrible and the school strange. Once again, she found it difficult to make friends, but she was amazingly happy in her new environment. The big city offered so much interest and a never-ending supply of fun activities, which more than compensated for what she had lost in the move.

Rationing had just been completely lifted, and the family gorged on sweets, chocolate and cake. The shops were beginning to fill with a plethora of goods for sale and an air of optimism spread through the country, which was headed by a new Queen. The towns were being rebuilt to replace the bombed-out ruins. Emily's father was a Londoner and loved his city, and each weekend, he would take her to see different areas. They would search for treasure on the small, exposed beaches of the Thames when the tide was out and wander around old churches and cathedrals. A regular was climbing the twisting stairway of the Monument to gaze at the view and also the Whispering Gallery of St Paul's Cathedral with its strange echoes. She had a smart grey coat with a matching hat with an upturned brim. Her father would take her to Trafalgar Square, fill the brim of her hat with birdseed and the pigeons would come flocking to eat their fill, settling on her shoulders, arms and hands. They were surprisingly heavy but she would laugh with delight and beg for more seed.

Within a few months, her parents had managed to buy a house in a nearby area, and the move was smooth. Emily was delighted to see the back of the unremitting brown décor. Her mother quickly ensured that the woodwork in the new home was painted white, cheerful curtains covered the windows, and the walls were any colour other than brown.

The house had the added advantage of being very close to the local park where all the kids from the surrounding streets congregated after school, weekends and holidays. It was not large but had all that was necessary to make life fun and exciting. It had a playground, tennis courts and a putting green where a modest sum could be spent giving a full hour of enjoyment trying to putt the ball into the very small hole. Emily managed to win quite a few games with her friends after many hours of practice. Roller skates were also a bonus, whizzing down the fairly steep slopes and trying not to crash into a tree when you reached the bottom. She never did manage to learn the art of safe stopping. Then there were the large areas of lawns for lolling around and eating junk and drinking fizzy pop. Many hours were spent in this verdant delight and at weekends, the children would sit around watching the larger kids playing football or the local cricket club in their whites on a Saturday afternoon.

Yet another new school beckoned close by to their home, and Emily could walk there by herself. Thanks to old connections of her father, she had a free place in a private prep school and she was overwhelmed by the wealth of the children there. Their clothing was luxurious, their downtown spent in expensive hobbies and extra-curricular activities, and once again Emily found herself on the periphery. She was not unhappy, however, and managed to make a few friends. Academically, there were no problems and the small classes ensured targeted attention from the teacher who liked and encouraged her. Emily thrived educationally and quickly rose to the top of the class despite having come from abroad so recently.

This grounding led to a straightforward trajectory to the local grammar school where she made friends, even if she was not one of the most popular among the girls, though still well-liked, in this single-sex school. Her extreme shyness continued to hold her back in this respect. As in her early years, she was unable to break the barrier which would permit her to understand and become part of the groups of girls who laughed and giggled and gossiped their way through the school playtimes, their arms round each other. It certainly had not helped that she had attended so many schools within a few short years in two different countries, making social interaction even more problematic. Just as in her junior school in the old country she was forced into a more solitary life outside the mainstream of girlish friendship. She turned to her drawing and the local library instead. Despite this she managed to make a couple of close friends.

Life in London for a serious child such as Emily held definite advantages. She was also fortunate to have parents who loved the cultural side of living in the capital and took advantage of all that such a major city had to offer. Many visits took place to the art galleries, theatres and concert halls. The local theatre each year held a month of Gilbert and Sullivan operettas, which her father so enjoyed, and he would take them to see each and every one, until they knew the libretto by heart. Opera and ballet were part and parcel of her life, but also pantomime each year where her father would embarrass them by shouting out the necessary, such as 'he's behind you', and she would try to hide from embarrassment and pretend she was not with him!

Of course, her very favourites were the art galleries where she would study the paintings carefully and sometimes try to copy them. The lives of the artists and their history fascinated her and she would go to the library and take out all their books on art, dragging the heavy volumes home in a bag on the bus. For some reason, she was only allowed, by library regulations, to take books out of the junior library until she was 14. By age 10, she had totally exhausted this library, but the head librarian, who had watched her over the years, gave her a special dispensation to use the adult section. This opened up a whole new world of art and literature to her.

Academic success led to a new growth in self-confidence. Maybe she could not hold her own with a whole group of chattering girls, but she gained kudos for her drawing and ability with a pencil. She was much in demand to help with geography homework with its dependence on drawing an accurate map. Before assembly on geography days, she would spend time drawing maps for many of the girls in her class who were unable to achieve success in this themselves. Didn't the teacher notice the similarity of the maps drawn by the class? Nothing was said, and she continued doing these favours for the other members of the class. Other classmates helped her with chemistry homework, which Emily hated. It was a quid pro quo, and all came out well from it. She was certainly contented in this environment.

The school building was state-of-the-art, with all modern facilities and excellent sports facilities spread over the large grounds which surrounded the school. The best part was in the summer when the girls were on their lunch break and they could lie spread out on the grass, soaking up the sun; their skirts hitched up as far as they dared so the sun could tan their white legs with a beautiful golden colour. They helped this along by slathering their legs with oil; any oil would do. No-one knew the dangers of skin cancer yet.

Emily's life outside of the school day was also very satisfactory. Although she really had little in common with her brother, who was still his mother's favourite, they did each have a group of friends whose social life interacted. His group was only boys. Hers was mixed in equal numbers. Her home was the epicentre. Their mother was a great baker and loved nothing more than to have their big dining table piled high with cakes, scones and pancakes on a Saturday afternoon. All the young crowd would gather round to eat the goodies, and her mother stayed tactfully out of sight. Did Emily appreciate all that her mother did for her on these occasions? Of course, she didn't!

They were a clever bunch of kids and the conversation veered from the banal to the sublime, touching on pop music to Freud, from musical theatre to evolution. The sixties were swinging and they lived in London, its heart and soul. All this new demographic of 'teenagers' took full advantage of the new society, but they did stop short of getting into the drug scene, which was growing rapidly. Neither did they smoke. Maybe they were a dull lot in that they did not become immured in the underbelly of the new era. Nevertheless, they enjoyed life to the full. They went to parties where the music throbbed, shaking the walls, tottering home in the small hours, belting out the latest No. 1 in the pop charts. Nightclubs were spreading, and they would have a change of scene at folk clubs in steamy, smoky basements in Swiss Cottage, joining in choruses of Good Night Irene at the tops of their voices. The Beatles and The Rolling Stones ruled.

Emily and some of her friends managed to get tickets for a Beatles concert in London. They arrived and sat in the middle stalls and the Beatles ran onto the stage with their instruments. A huge roar erupted as the audience started to scream in a frenzy of devotion and fervour. They stood up and threw items at the stage, and the Beatles played on. Anyway, Emily presumed they carried on, but as they left the venue at the end of the show, they had to admit that they had absolutely no idea what had been sung as the screaming had been so extreme. It was also a good hour before they could actually discuss the concert, as they had all been rendered completely deaf by the ear-piercing cacophony.

The saying goes that 'if you remember the sixties, you weren't actually there'. This is definitely false. Emily and her friends were always to remember the sixties, and that was certainly better than being lost in a drug-induced fog or alcoholic vacuum.

And then there were the clothes and here Emily came into her element. She loved fashion, designing it, wearing it and making a big statement. She was good with her hands and each week, she would sew herself a new outfit of her own design. She would embellish these sometimes with embroidery or sequins. Hems would be high and boots long and shiny. Carnaby Street and The Kings Road were the mecca for all the latest gear. These were completed with the extravagant make-up made popular by the revolutionary Mary Quant and pop idols such as Dusty Springfield. Max Factor produced a block of eye liner in a neat blue box, which came complete with a tiny brush. Emily would wet the block with a bit of spit, rub the brush in the moistened blackness and apply it carefully to her eyelids, curving out to a sweeping arch up and outwards. One could not forget the hairdo, backcombed and high and then stuck firmly in place with a blast of hairspray.

The first time she appeared before her parents in her bright red pleated mini-skirt, she descended the stairs to find them at the bottom gazing at her. They looked hard at her but said nothing except for an 'enjoy yourself'. She was so impressed with their sang-froid at this totally new look. She sailed out of the house in her finery into a new society which promised such a golden future.

All this activity was undertaken with the radio blaring the latest pop music in the background. Only the BBC was allowed to broadcast at this time, and so 'pirate boats' took to the seas outside the three-mile limit, which allowed companies such as Radio Luxembourg and Radio Caroline to beam endless music to the shores of England. The latest songs were interspersed with adverts, which were not permitted on the BBC. At school the next day, kids would discuss the latest offerings, and they would choose which vinyl records to buy to play on their Dansette record players.

The boys discovered Emily. Emily did not give them much thought, considering them a necessary evil. However, she was a very pretty girl, petite and slim, with long wavy hair. When she was small, her mother would brush it each morning and then plait it with brightly coloured ribbons. The refrain was always the same: 'what a shame you have such mousy hair. Mine was such a pretty colour'. As a result, Emily was totally unaware of her own attractiveness and would check her hair in the mirror but always was relatively happy with what she saw and could not understand the criticism. The thought always lingered that, obviously, her 'crowning glory' was not so crowning after all. This undermining of her confidence was constant and would lead to further problems for her throughout the years. There were never to be any compliments from her mother – ever.

She was, therefore, somewhat taken aback when boys started to take notice of her. She and her friends never discussed the other sex, nor did they talk about weddings and wedding dresses. The magazines designed for young teens were pretty coy about the facts of life, alluding rather than explaining. She was totally ignorant of this aspect of life, which was an issue never to be discussed by her mother or father. There definitely was no sex education in schools. Somehow, she had discovered what she needed to know, maybe by osmosis, or maybe her friends had discussed these matters. Emily had no recollection. The sixties arrived with a blast to change the sexual scene forever. The new contraceptive pill not only gave women a totally new freedom but opened up the discussion of the place of women in society. The job market would also widen opportunities, but nonetheless, this was not the experience of all women.

It was difficult to ascertain who was more frightened: the boys summoning up the courage to ask her out or Emily's ability to respond. Her continuing shyness and lack of self-confidence made her turn down many offers of outings with attractive boys of similar age. When she did consent, she was unsure how to respond and how to behave on the date. She was paralysed with diffidence. Gradually, as more boys circled around her, she began to lose her reticence, and the odd date morphed into a relationship of sorts. Sex was definitely not on the agenda, but Emily got the impression that the boys were even more frightened of that aspect than she was herself. Although the pill was now a welcome reality, it was not readily available to the general public outside of marriage. The sexual life of the young was still somewhat problematic.

By the time her sixteenth birthday arrived, life was definitely on a roll. She was popular with boys and girls alike, and school was a doddle. She worked hard but was well rewarded in her public exams, which came easily to her. She was definitely not a genius but a good all-rounder on most subjects which she encountered. Emily looked forward to university, followed by a career which would give her satisfaction together with financial reward. These would allow her to live independently from her family, unfettered by the parental chains that were so tight about her.

Emily quickly realised, despite the new exciting culture which surrounded her, that the world was divided into two distinct groups. There were those who were ready to rebel, to throw off the shackles which had bound their mothers and grandmothers and embrace the new liberty. Then there was a sizable group who did not have the courage to go counter to their parents' wishes and saw the new autonomy with trepidation and fear. Emily was definitely of the latter group. She was living through an era of great change, particularly for women, but many were cautious to grab the new opportunities which were becoming a possibility. They were on the cusp of a new world but it would be many years developing, often at a snail's pace with every forward step fought for long and hard.

She loved her parents and they were devoted to her, as long as she toed the party line. They were stuck in their Victorian past, where there were distinct roles to be played by boys and those to be pursued by girls. Boys were to be highly educated and prepared for careers and work. Girls were to marry, produce offspring and prepare wholesome meals for their hardworking husbands on their return each night. By ensuring she had a wonderful education, they would deprive her of her full potential and ensure a life of misery; of this, no-one was aware of at the time. She saw the promised land but could not cross the river to stand on its further shore.

Despite being a high flyer at school, every avenue she explored for a career and proposed course at university was turned down without discussion by her parents.

"I want to go to university. I really want to study history in more depth and then maybe teach," she told her parents.

"What would be the point? You're only going to get married and start a family. Who is going to look after your children while you're going off to a job each day? It's out of the question. You need to be more realistic. Do a secretarial course. It was good enough for me, it will be good enough for you," her mother replied.

Emily was furious. She knew her parents did not need help with the family finances. By this time, her father had created a successful business. The old-fashioned attitudes of her parents, who were still of the belief that 'children should be seen but not heard' precluded Emily from arguing her corner. This, and her naturally cautious nature, also stopped her from taking the rebellious route. Her highly academic school was of no help and did virtually nothing to ensure that their clever alumni furthered their education. Her headmistress told her that 'she washed her hands of her' when Emily informed her she definitely did not want a career as a nurse or primary school teacher. That was the sum total of career preparation at the school.

It did not seem to appear to the headmistress that there was something of a dichotomy here. She, the successful career woman, head of a large grammar school had advanced through university and worked her way up through all the rungs of the ladder to the highest echelons. Yet she was advising academic, clever girls to go for jobs which required minimum academic qualifications and to eschew the route of university and head higher so that they could achieve their potential. Would she mentor boys in the same way? Emily doubted it. As her brother disappeared into the university system for a total of seven years, she was enrolled in the dreaded secretarial course, destined to slave away in a soul-destroying boring office working for men who were definitely not up to the job, but they were men, weren't they?

Emily's social life kept her happy and motivated. Boyfriends came and went, but she always felt somewhat separate from them, and they faded out with no ill will on either side. She continued to make her gorgeous clothes with speed and precision and designed herself in the trendy style fashionable then. There were parties, many held in her own home, which went on until the early hours.

Unknown numbers of friends would stay the night, sleeping wherever they could. Her easy-going mother, so old-fashioned in some respect, would come down in the morning asking 'how many for breakfast today?' How could she be so up-to-date in some ways but unable to see that the world had moved on from the 1920s and 30s?

Definitely, there were problems for Emily. But problems can be solved, can't they?

CHAPTER 4

She swung down the street, her bag flung over her shoulder and her long hair flowing behind her and lifted by the breeze. The leaves on the street trees were unfurling their colors, a pale lime green that would darken with the passing of the months. The pavement was already dappled by the shade caused by the sun filtering through their canopies. Wolf whistles followed her in a wave of sound, but she loftily ignored them, although she would cast a sneaky sideward glance to see who it was casting covetous eyes at her. Who could resist? The London streets were heaving with pedestrians out and about on their daily business, window shopping, gossiping at corners and sitting in cafes deep in conversation or just watching the world go by. The traffic lurched by in its usual jerky fashion, brought to a halt every few yards by traffic lights, snarl-ups or zebra crossings. Getting anywhere in London by car was well-nigh impossible, and those walking soon overtook the cars with their big engines emitting fumes and going nowhere very slowly.

The sun was shining, the overnight rain having finally cleared in the early hours. As long as you could discount the traffic exhaust fumes, the air felt fresh and new born under the blue sky, which was only lightly flecked with fluffy white clouds. The gentlest of breezes caressed her skin with a gentle warmth of kindness. The busy shopping street was a kaleidoscope of colour, a tapestry of fun from the summery dresses of the girls. Their skirts were short, some so skimpy they were barely visible, and their long-tanned legs ended with platform strappy sandals. They were a joy to behold. Emily's appearance fits nicely with that of the other girls in the street. A slim-fitting grass-green mini dress showed off her slender figure, and a loose chain belt made up of large golden rings accentuated her tiny waist. Long, shiny PVC boots finished the look together with a large, white shoulder bag, which swung from side to side as she walked resolutely down the street. Many of the young men were almost as peacock-like. The short back and sides had long gone, and hair was almost as long as Emily's, often tied back in a pony tail or trailing down to their shoulders. From the back, it was impossible to say if it was male or female. Their clothes, too, had undergone a total transformation in the last few years. No longer the formal jacket and tie but rather tie-dyed T-shirts and flared denim jeans. They were definitely sartorial competition for the girls. They were certainly keen competition in the clothing department and gave the street a glamorous and stimulating vibrancy.

Emily was meeting her friend Suzanne for lunch. They were meeting in a small vegetarian restaurant, down some stairs in a basement off Oxford Street. Such restaurants were just beginning to proliferate but were definitely the exception rather than commonplace. Emily liked it because of the unusual salads and the plentiful use of vegetables combined with fruit, which she was used to from her early childhood. Only now was London starting to catch up with international cuisine and beginning to lose its dire reputation for tasteless, bland dining. She would regularly see a well-known DJ there who would bring famous pop stars with him, but everyone would ignore them and let them eat in peace and quiet.

The two girls caught up on all the news they had since last speaking the evening before. There was always plenty to gossip about. Suzanne, always Suzanne and never Suzie (she hated anyone shortening her name), also had an office job but was progressing well up the corporate ladder in the marketing department of her company. She definitely looked the epitome of the successful business worker in her well-cut grey suit, the skirt stopping quite a bit above the knees with trendy ankle boots. She had a white formal shirt on, the collar unbuttoned, with French cuffs and big shiny silver cuff links peeping out from the sleeves of her jacket.

She wore her mass of dark curly hair piled up with two large combs holding it in place and long, dangly silver earrings. Her face was carefully made up with lots of dramatic eye make-up, which was so fashionable at the moment. She rather enjoyed the work she was doing and saw a good future there. She was outgoing and sassy and could hold her own in the lively office environment, easily batting off the continual sexual innuendoes launched at her by the male workers. The two girls looked marvellous, and all heads turned in their direction as they took their seats in the busy dining room. They pretended not to notice but gave each other a small sideways smile of satisfaction at the stir they were causing.

They found themselves a table tucked well into the corner, checked out the menu and put in their orders for a healthy salad with regard to their waistlines but with a side of chips just for the heck of it. They set about their food and soon meandered onto a favourite topic of theirs – getting away from home and discovering the big, wide world. The two of them had been thrashing around this subject for many years, lolling around on their beds and listening to records and munching chocolate bars while they moaned and grumbled about their boring, miserable lives.

"Isn't it time we stopped talking and maybe did something about this?" Suzanne suggested.

"You're right. I'm really fed up with living at home. There are so many dos and don'ts all the time. ' You're living in my house, so you'll do what I say,'" Emily mimicked her father.

"Then it's time we stopped talking about it and actually did something positive; otherwise, it will never happen, and we'll be stuck with our parents forever. We really need to be more proactive and make a final push to get away and lead our own lives. But how to go about it and make it happen?"

"Can you imagine what the parents will say, though? The disgrace; how can I hold my head up? What will people say?" Suzanne held her head in her hands. "Terrible things will happen. Two girls sharing a flat in the city can only lead to catastrophe. I never thought that they would be so thoughtless and cruel. Haven't they given any thought to our feelings?"

Emily laughed and nodded in agreement, nibbling thoughtfully on a wholemeal bread roll and considering their options.

The sixties were a time of innovation, discovery and brand-new freedom, yet there was still great conflict about girls leaving home before marriage. Marriage was the ideal, the promised land. Work was considered just a stop-gap between school and the trip to the altar. Despite the cultural and social revolution that was taking place, many were left behind in the old traditions and universities, and careers still did not beckon. The world was a male hierarchy, and even though many girls were now well educated to a high level, the workplace was not open to them. The patriarchal society made sure of that. A girl would need determination and a great deal of luck to break through the very powerful glass ceiling that prevented advancement in the workplace. Even if a girl did manage to rise in the workplace, her salary would be pitched lower than her male equivalent. She also had to constantly run the gauntlet of harassment and sexual abuse to a greater or lesser degree. It was such a minefield and rampant in just about every office. Having the support of one's family was a practical and psychological advantage. Emily and Suzanne lacked this totally and neither was able to push themselves forward due to their old-fashioned families and lack of self-confidence to shatter the mould they had been born into.

The gap year was unknown, and Suzanne and Emily were both aware that making such a move to break the cords of home living would not be popular with their families. And that was putting it mildly. Such a breakout would need to be carefully planned and actioned. They were determined to buck the trend and not be sidelined into the stultifying corner of domesticity and dirty nappies. The general trend for making an escape was for followers of the Beatles to trek up to the Himalayas or similar places in order to find a guru who would give them enlightenment and teach them the secrets of existence while they sat cross-legged at his feet, nodding wisely in agreement. This gave these youngsters the opportunity to smoke their weed or stronger, meditate and find the meaning of life and the universe. After a period of cogitation, they would descend from the mountain, hopefully in good health or alternatively with a bad psychotic episode due to the over-indulgence of narcotic highs.

This was not for Emily and Suzanne. They had other plans. Leaving home was high on their list and a top priority. They were both working, albeit in monotonous, boring jobs, but earning quite good salaries, and both had stashed away a decent amount of money in their savings accounts.

"What we need is to really get away from home. Find a flat together. Live our own lives the way we want to without our parents breathing down our necks at every turn," Suzanne stated. "Wouldn't it be amazing not to have to be answerable for everything we say or do? Not to have to be in by a certain time or creep in like little mice when we come home really late so as not to get an earful in the morning."

"My dad bangs a stick on the floor of his bedroom when he hears me with a boy downstairs late at night. It's mortifying, it really is. Then, sometimes, he appears in his dressing gown and just sits down in his armchair and glowers. Doesn't say a word. How embarrassing!"

"How do we go about it then? Can you imagine their reaction when we tell them our plans? We also don't have much money, though I've managed to save quite a bit. What about you?" They started to discuss the matter in more detail. The flat would have to be small and cheap but clean. As they talked about it, their excitement mounted and they spun castles in the air as they anticipated how life would be in their own small property well away from the prying eyes of their loving families. It would be such bliss! Just think!

They were under no illusions. "It's not going to be easy. It's going to be tight financially, but let's work out how much we would need each month. What are the big money bills? We need to make a list to see what's what."

"Then we would also have to do all the cleaning, shopping and cooking with no mothers to dance attendance on us. We certainly wouldn't be taking home the washing for mummy to do. Can you imagine their faces if we tried that? Mind you, my brother used to do that when he was at uni. It's all right for him, though. One rule for the boys and a totally different one for the girls. This emancipation lark is certainly taking its time to penetrate our homes. Let's try and work it out then, we would have some idea if we could actually make this work. We need pen and paper to get down to some serious calculations."

None of their friends had left home. They were going to be trailblazers. Maybe they would start a trend. Would they be able to do all the things necessary; hold down a full-time job, and still have time and money for a social life? Suzanne and Emily talked away the afternoon while the waiter kept the cups of coffee coming. Their parents would be furious. Their Victorian attitudes would not permit such permissiveness, which is how they would see their erring offspring's behaviour. The two girls discussed this part of their plan carefully and came to the conclusion that every aspect of their ambition had to be fully put in place with no chance of backtracking before they could come clean to their families. They set to work.

"Can we afford London?"

"We have no other option. Our jobs are here. I don't want to move to the provinces and leave all we have here in London. It's all happening here. The provinces are oh-so provincial! And wages are much lower there."

"You're right. Boring….."

They took out a notebook and started jotting down figures and numbers, trying to anticipate the costs they would incur running their own small domain, which would obviously be split between the two of them. There was the rent, of course. That was the big one. Then there were Council Rates, electricity, gas and food. They added up the sums and their combined salaries, working out how much they needed for travel and social life. The numbers seemed to add up – just. It was definitely doable. They smiled at each other and hugged in celebration and parted company to return to their respective offices and a somewhat truncated afternoon of yet more dull routine.

Now, they just needed to put their plan into action.

The first item on the agenda was, of course, finding somewhere to live. They obviously realised that upmarket areas would be well out of their price bracket so they decided to check out the cheaper boroughs. There was a limit on how low they were willing to sink in the housing market. They needed to feel safe, able to walk home from the station or bus at night without fearing for their lives. There were parts of this large city which were notoriously rough and dangerous. Both of them had been brought up in the genteel outer suburbs where street violence was not an issue. They also had to prepare themselves psychologically to face the reality of inner-city living. They discussed their requirements and also what they would definitely not tolerate. They would draw a red line which would not be crossed.

"We need to get hold of the evening papers each day, look in the property section and see what is available to rent," Suzanne said decisively. "The alternative is to go to estate agents, but you have to find the one for the area you want. I think the papers would be easier, don't you."

"I really hope that it doesn't take us too long to find a place. I just want to move out from my parents' place, much as I love them. But you hear such horror stories of people trying to find somewhere to live, and some places are so grotty. It's not going to be easy," Emily countered.

Flats, they knew, were at a premium, London was buzzing, and demand was high. It was not going to be easy. It was not so long in the past that the Prime Minister had informed the public that 'they had never had it so good'. "We'll really need to put all our efforts into this and need to be persistent. I don't think it's going to be a walkover finding something suitable," Emily continued.

They paid the bill and parted to go back to their respective jobs. Emily darted down the steps to the Underground, picking up the two evening papers, which would be the start of her search. Suzanne would be doing likewise. The 'for rent' section was quite considerable and needed careful studying of the jargon which would give clues to the property. 'Bijou' meant you couldn't turn around in the flat. 'Needs some work' was giving you to understand that the paint was flaking from the walls, together with rising damp and the cupboard doors hanging off their hinges. 'Convenient for restaurants' was another way of saying there was a fish and chip shop underneath the flat wafting huge drafts of vinegar and frying oil stench up into your home. These would seriously reduce the number of suitable properties. They would definitely need to remain upbeat and not become disheartened if the hunt were to be protracted.

The journey home passed in a flash as she studied the paper. She tucked it in her bag, with the 'flats available' section well hidden from prying eyes. She certainly would have to keep it well under wraps from the laser eyes of her parents. There was a long way to go before she could reveal her intentions to them. In fact, it might take a long time to explore available properties before an appropriate one can be located.

Dinner was over. It had been hard keeping her plans and excitement to herself as she tried to keep her face from reflecting the excitement she felt inside, but her parents seemed to suspect nothing. Emily finally took herself up to her bedroom to check out the paper again for suitable flats, glad to leave the tension she was feeling probably imaginary. She circled a few hopefuls and started on the arduous task of phoning around to organise viewings. Some hope. All had gone within minutes. This was definitely going to be even more difficult than she and Suzanne had anticipated, and they realised that they would have to get hold of the paper the moment it hit the streets to be in with any chance of success.

Tomorrow was another day, and lessons had been learned. This was going to be a steep learning curve, but they would win out in the end. They just had to learn to play the system; they and thousands of other people longed to live independently. They had to be one step ahead of the hordes to be in with any chance of success and be prepared to move fast if anything reasonable became available. There could be no procrastinating.

Between them, Emily and Suzanne scoured the papers each day, made phone calls and even saw some properties. Both were determined to succeed, and the stronger-willed Suzanne managed to motivate her friend to keep up the search and the motivation. It was all very depressing. There were properties where you could barely get into the communal hallway because of rubbish piled up. In one, rented by some students, they could not go into the kitchen as even the floor was completely covered with dirty plates, food containers and an impossibly high number of cups and mugs, all filthy dirty. Others were so dark you needed the lights on all day, and yet more, which were just plain revolting; just the thought of the clean-up required made them non-starters. They even saw a couple which came with resident livestock!

They were persistent, however, and eventually saw a small flat on the first floor of a converted Victorian house in a tree-lined street close to the Underground and within a sensible walk of the shops. They would have to share a bedroom, but the living room was high-ceiling and had lovely original features. It must have been a beautiful home before some rich landlord carved up the property to make many small flats and earn even more money. The kitchen was pokey, of course, but they didn't anticipate hosting huge dinner parties. Entertaining would have to be on an informal basis with finger food and takeaways.

The flat was furnished but they could buy what they needed extra from the Salvation Army or second-hand shops. Hopefully, once their parents were over the shock of their little darlings leaving home, they would contribute linen, crockery and other necessities. They signed the lease. They were now on the road to independence. It was simultaneously frightening and exciting. They hugged and laughed, anticipating the shenanigans about to explode in their direction.

The fun was just beginning. Now, they had to break the news to their parents.

"We have to do it at the same time."

"I agree. They are bound to get on the phone with each other. I think there will be a lot of screaming and shouting."

"After dinner tonight? Say 8 o'clock?" They looked at each other and smiled, conspirators with a dream. The two girls discussed tactics and a plan of action. They knew the coming confrontation would be long and hard, but they would have to stand firm if they were to get their way.

Emily sat at the table that evening, trembling all over as she attempted to pluck up the subject of her intention to flee the bosom of her family in a desperate bid for freedom. She took a deep breath and decided to dive straight in. However, she did this, knowing trouble lay just ahead.

"I've made a decision," she stammered. "Suzanne and I have made plans to move into a flat of our own. We've found a place to rent and signed the contract…"

Total silence. Her parents looked totally confused, she realised. They had not seen this coming at all and were obviously not taking in what she had said.

"I'm moving out." she repeated. "The time has come for me to stand on my own two feet and try and discover for myself what I want out of life. I know I need space and independence for this to happen." She was babbling now, having lost the thread of her argument and realising that she had dived in with no careful thought or consideration. She ploughed on. "I know this is a huge move, especially for you to take on board. But you've brought me up with all the right values, and I also know that you want the best for me according to your beliefs that a girl should stay at home until she marries, going from one protected environment straight into another. I really don't want that. I need to find myself and move away from this Victorian way of life. Times have changed, and so has the position of young women. Suzanne and I are both responsible. We won't get into drugs or drink. We won't get into trouble just because we're not living under our parents' roofs. We'll definitely be okay." She came to a halt, seeing the colour in her father's face rising to a scary purple, just waiting to explode. Obviously, she had gone about things the wrong way. But she also knew that there was no 'right way'.

The tension mounted as her father prepared to start his onslaught. Her mother looked as though she was about to burst into tears.

"Where did this come from?" he suddenly exploded at a full bellow. "What on earth are you thinking of? This will be a disaster. And you didn't think to discuss this in any way. Just dived in head first, in total secrecy. Is this what we have taught you? To be devious and underhand? None of our friends have this situation to deal with. They are going to be shocked, and we will have to live with the shame and embarrassment of our daughter going off the rails like this. You have to cancel the contract and forget all about this mad scheme of yours. And I would have thought your friend would have more sense. I'm totally upset at your behaviour and thoughtlessness."

"We're not living in times gone by. This is the twentieth century, and things have changed, but you seem to have noticed nothing of what is happening around you," she retorted. "This is going to happen. I'm sorry. I don't want to upset you or hurt you, but I can't live my life for the sake of what your friends will think. This is my life and my future, and I want to shape it for myself. I've done everything you wanted till now, but it's a done deal. I'm moving out and I really would prefer to do it with your blessing and support."

The meal that evening had certainly taken a turn for the worse. As she had known would happen, her very old-fashioned parents considered it a disgrace that their beloved and much-cherished baby was making a bid for freedom. Their friends would be shocked and feel pity for them that they could not control their child. She had said her piece, and now she just had to hold fast and not be bullied into their way of thinking.

"This is a lot for you to take in," she went on "but really, we will not be raped, attacked or robbed. We're both level-headed and sensible. It will work out. I know that, and we won't be living any kind of wild life. Just our own lives, in our own way, in our own space."

"Times have changed," she said. "We're living in the nineteen sixties, not the eighteenth century. I'll tell you how I feel, shall I? I feel like a parcel, wrapped in brown paper and tied up with string, despatched from your ownership to that of the man I'm supposed to marry. Well, I'm not just a package to be passed from one male to another. I'm determined to throw away the wrapping and decide my own life in my own way. I'm doing this whatever you say, but I would prefer your support."

There was silence while the three of them sat and considered their next move. Emily was distraught. She hated scenes, and this was definitely the worst fall-out she had ever had with her parents, but she knew she had to stand firm, or matters would never change.

The phone rang, breaking into the tense silence. As expected, Suzanne's parents were on the line; their rage was so great that it really didn't require the intervention of a telephone line. The two sets of parents commiserated with each other about how the world was going to the dogs and that the youth of today were selfish and out of control. This would never have happened in their day. Where had they gone so wrong? Eventually, they talked themselves dry, stared at their daughters and realised that they were in the throes of a battle which they could not win. Emily and Suzanne were implacable.

The girls would move into their new home that weekend.

CHAPTER 5

They made a tour of their new domain, not that it took very long. One bedroom, one living room with a table at the end and one bathroom. It was definitely small but all their own. They placed the furniture in different positions in the good-sized lounge until they found an acceptable layout and discussed cleaning rotas and other practicalities. At first, it was like playing 'house'. Sure enough, just as they had thought, their mothers were the first to face reality with an approach of 'if you can't beat them, then you may as well join them', and they came up trumps with spare linen, china and glassware. They stocked up their fridge and cupboards to make sure their daughters would not starve to death for lack of food. How would they explain their daughters' brainstorm to their friends?

Playing house for real was totally unlike the make-believe of their early childhood with a toy kitchen, pretend food and dolls sitting in a circle. Now, the reality of holding down a full-time job plus running a home, however small, entailed planning and hard work. Cleaning, shopping and cooking did not happen by itself and there was much to learn. They had watched their mothers over the years, and it had all looked so easy, but cooking, especially, was something of a minefield. Food was burnt, meals were undercooked and many a meal hit the bin. There was much experimentation, but they started to learn and managed to prepare some actually very decent menus, much to their surprise and pleasure.

It was enjoyable having friends around without having to worry about their parents in the bedroom upstairs. Music could be played at all hours, and even the housework, if not actually enjoyable, was done in the spirit of fun. Friends would regularly knock on the door, clutching a bottle of wine; the record player would be piled high with records, and talk went on till the early hours. The only downside was having to clear the mess up at the end of the evening because neither one of them could bear going into the living room first thing in the morning to be faced with dirty glasses, plates strewn with now congealed food and a light dusting of crisp crumbs decorating the carpet. Maybe they could lay down rules to their guests that crisps should go down throats and not be scattered like confetti through every room. Their friends didn't seem to have the same problem with their alcohol. Not a drop of that was ever wasted or spilt!

The two girls soon discovered the faults in each other but learned to adapt. Suzanne had the habit of piling her clothes on the chair at the foot of her bed as she took them off at night. The pile would grow higher and higher, and it was possible to work out what she had worn each day for the previous umpteen weeks. Then, one day, the mountain of clothes would grow so tall and precarious that the whole lot would topple over, covering the floor. This was the impetus she needed to either put them in the wash or hang them up, mainly because she had run out of clean clothes to wear!

Emily, on the other hand, found difficulty in clearing the sink of washed dishes so there was always a dangerous load piled high on the sink waiting to be put away. She was also somewhat obsessive about throwing things out. Suzanne would look for the magazine she had been saving to read at the weekend only to discover it had been binned days before. Never mind, they learned to live with the foibles and just laughed at each other, never arguing or having a crossword.

One evening, they had each invited some friends around for an impromptu party. They bought in some nibbles and plenty of drinks, such as wine, beer and soft drinks. Suzanne was bringing some friends she had made at work whom Emily had never met. She was looking forward to meeting them. She had heard of one guy from Suzanne who had recently broken up with his girlfriend, whom she thought Emily might like. She would wait and see.

Here he was. Tall and slim, nice looking, sparkling blue eyes gazed down at her from his towering height. His hair must have been blond at some point in his childhood but now was a medium brown but streaked with fair as though he had had it highlighted. He looked at Emily with interest, small and petite, although somewhat shy and reserved. His name was Marcus, he told her and proceeded to chat her up. He certainly did not lack self-confidence and seemed to have quite a high opinion of himself. Emily was less than impressed. He was not put off by her off-hand attitude and set about trying to curry favour with her. Maybe he tried so hard just because she lacked interest, or maybe he was unaware that he was not getting the feedback to spur him on. Although he tried hard, Emily was not prepared just to fall at his feet and spent the evening chatting with one and all, not excluding Marcus entirely. He did not give up, though, and kept appearing at her side to gain her attention.

The evening ended, the clearing up took place, and the next day beckoned with work and the routine of earning a living.

The next evening, the phone rang, and Suzanne took the call.

"Emily, it's for you."

Emily took up the receiver and heard the voice from the previous night.

"Hi, it's Marcus. It was great meeting you last night. It was really enjoyable talking to you and I wondered if you would like to meet me at the weekend, maybe go for a walk and out for coffee and cake. I would like to get to know you better," he said.

She was somewhat taken aback by the offer, but although she had not really taken it to him, she had little on that weekend, and maybe it would be pleasant to have an afternoon out. He won full marks for persistence, as she had certainly not paid him much attention the previous evening. He did look very presentable, however. The weather was going to be sunny and warm, so what had she to lose?

"That sounds like a nice idea" she replied.

"Good. I'll pick you up at 3."

The day arrived, and Emily dressed carefully. She wanted to impress him but not to appear too eager. It was a careful balancing act, and as she looked at herself in the long mirror in the bedroom, she was happy with what she saw. Her long hair was shiny and wavy and fell to her shoulders. Her makeup was light but casual, and she wore a bright cotton skirt teamed with a toning sleeveless top. She finished off the ensemble with dangly brightly coloured earrings and a small gold chain around her throat. Flat blue espadrilles completed the look.

"You look gorgeous," he said upon seeing her come out the door. Good start, she thought and smiled as she climbed next to him into the car. He, too, had obviously made an effort in a casual/smart style, which she thought really suited him. She had to admit that he certainly was very attractive, and she started to re-assess her initial opinion of him.

The afternoon was fun. She had to acknowledge that. The first time she met him, he seemed overbearing and rather full of himself, but now she realised he had probably been somewhat nervous and had become carried away by overcompensating. Now he was more relaxed, asking her all about herself and obviously wanting to learn more about her. He definitely was good company, amusing and intelligent.

"I really enjoyed this afternoon. I think you're really gorgeous, clever and good company. Would you come out with me again soon, maybe for a meal later this week?"

"You know. That's a great idea. I have to say I really had fun today. Maybe we could meet on Wednesday evening?"

The relationship grew and progressed. The chemistry was very powerful. They would meet at the weekend and once or twice during the week. They found much in common in a love of music. There were so many wonderful groups and singers doing the rounds, and they loved to go to different venues to hear them perform live. London was buzzing and the place to be, especially if you were young. Endless opportunities and choices were everywhere around to have fun. The theatre was another mutual love but more of an occasional treat due to the cost. Restaurants cooking food from around the world were now to be found opening all over the town, and it was great sourcing a new cuisine and trying it out. She and Marcus were definitely a couple now, and their friends automatically invited them together. When funds were low, they would investigate one of the parks, different at each season, so always a source of beauty and exercise, a long walk finished with a hot drink at the park café, sitting on a bench and watching all the other couples, parents with their youngsters and old people strolling by.

She even took him to meet her parents, who seemed to like him! She had, however, not met his parents yet, although she had come across his two brothers. Marcus still lived at home, which was a big house in a nice suburb with expensive cars in the drive. From what Marcus said, his parents had big plans for him and his brothers and their expectations were high. They sounded, his father especially, very controlling.

"I really don't understand. What's your parents' problems with me? They can't dislike someone they have never met. What do they say?"

"I'm not sure but let's give it some time. I'm sure they'll come round in the not-too-distant future." Emily decided not to pursue the matter for now. She would just play the waiting game and hope the issue would resolve itself, given some time. There were solutions for most problems. She was enjoying herself and wondered whether this was true love. The only fly in the ointment was definitely his parents' attitude towards meeting her, or rather, not meeting her.

The months rolled on, and life was a joy. Marcus was good for her. His attention and devotion to her helped bring her out of her shell, and she grew in self-confidence, something that had always eluded her. Emily realised she was happy and tried not to think about her relationship with his parents. One of his brothers was somewhat cool towards her; the other was always warm and friendly. She found all this confusing and upsetting, and she could not understand the situation at all. What was wrong with her? After all, his parents had never even met her, so how could they form an opinion? They were from similar backgrounds and they discovered that the two fathers had even attended the same school. What was the problem? Marcus did not like to discuss the topic at all and assured her all would work out well in the end. She believed him.

Emily was fast approaching her twenty-first birthday, and she and Suzanne planned a big party to celebrate the occasion. Life could not be better. She had a secure job, a loving boyfriend, living in a flat she liked. Certainly, her job was boring, and she was not fulfilling her potential. She had plans to go to university as she should have done on leaving school, and she was looking into studying for a degree and attending lectures part-time while holding down a job. It would be hard work, but worth it in the end if she could achieve a proper career in a way that gave her satisfaction and pleasure. At present, her work was mundane and trivial. She wanted to give her brain a good workout. She would also hopefully manage to earn more money to improve her lifestyle.

Food was bought, drinks laid out and new outfits for the celebration found, paid for and set out in readiness. The excitement was mounting and fortunately, Emily's birthday fell on the weekend so there was no work to go to on the day, and the whole time could be spent organising and preparing for the big event. The postman had been, and a satisfying clunk on the doormat presupposed a large number of cards ready to be opened and placed on various surfaces. The doorbell rang and there was a florist with a large bouquet of pink roses from her parents. They were so beautiful, and she quickly found a suitable vase for them.

The doorbell rang again. "I'll go," Emily shouted and ran excitedly down the stairs to the front door to welcome the newcomer. She opened the door, but there was no one there. Strange... She looked up and down the street but saw no one. Then she looked down and there on the doorstep was a parcel and a card. Someone did not want to be seen. She took the package upstairs and opened what she thought would be a card. It was not a card. It was a letter, a long one, in Marcus's handwriting. She recognised the paper. It came from a posh writing set she had herself given him on his twenty-first birthday the previous year.

She unfolded the letter, and her eyes skimmed down the first page. Her eyes opened wide, not believing what she was reading. She read the words on the page again and a third time, though they were jumping about all over the place, blurring and illogical. He had dumped her. By letter, on the morning of her birthday. She was not good enough for him apparently, so thought his parents even though they had never ever met her, and for the last year, they had been nagging at him to end it with her. The tears filled her eyes but did not fall. She was in complete shock. What sort of person would do such a thing with such cruel timing? It was so unexpected. She honestly thought he would stand by her. The letter continued for three pages. Each page detailed yet another way in which she was not worthy of this young man. She had thought him strong and high-minded. He was not, just weak and easily manipulated. She opened the package. It was a state-of-the art radio, the latest design and very expensive. Conscience money.

Without saying a word, she wrapped up the package again, went outside and took the bus to his home where he lived with his parents. She was so furious and totally fired-up, and the adrenaline kept her that way until she reached his street. She found the house where she had never had the chance to visit and left the parcel on the front doorstep, rang the bell and quickly turned the corner from his street. She caught the next bus back to her flat, where a distraught Suzanne was waiting for her. The surge of fury had now totally dissipated, and now the tears began to flow down her cheeks, onto her clothes and dripped onto the floor in front of her. Her world had fallen apart suddenly and irreparably. Suzanne held her tight while her body continued to rack with her sobs.

"I can't believe this is happening. How could he do this to me today, of all days? What sort of bastard breaks up by letter on the day of your birthday? Couldn't he have waited till tomorrow? I think I'm in a ghastly nightmare. How could he be such a wimp after all his fine talk of loving me and standing by me? It was all nonsense, just a pack of lies. I feel so dirty and used. I'll never get over this. Never."

"It's hard to believe this of Marcus. I really thought he had more backbone than this. I'm just so sorry that this is happening to you. What is it with men? They just bluster and stampede their way through life, taking what they want and controlling every aspect of our lives. His timing is unbelievable. It's certainly a man's world, no doubt about it," Suzanne muttered, and then she remembered, "What shall we do now? What about the party?" she finally asked as Emily took a much-needed breath.

Emily looked at her in puzzlement. The party had completely fled her mind and now she again had to face the reality. Dozens of people were due in a couple of hours. There was no time to phone round as so many would already be en route.

“We have to go ahead. There’s no time to cancel, is there?’ she said dully. The whole scenario filled her with horror. How would she survive an evening such as this? Tonight was to have been such a highlight in her life, a coming of age celebrated with those who cared and loved her. Her world had crashed about her into tiny smithereens like minute shards of glass piercing her skin and body, hurting and stabbing until her whole being felt on fire. The tears had flown so long and so hard that she felt utterly dehydrated and sick with exhaustion. She needed to find some extra resources from somewhere in order to get through the evening ahead, even though she was distraught and just wanted to hide away in her bed with the covers pulled over her head.

The evening passed in a blur of misery. It felt like an out-of-body experience. She was physically there and she heard herself chatting, talking to her friends. She heard the music, the congratulations, but nothing penetrated the thick armour enclosing her body in a tight grip. Her mind was filled with a thick fog like the terrible ones of her youth, which used to plague London every winter. What had happened quickly spread around the room. Long silences filled the air with their nothingness. Somebody turned the music up so high that the light fitting started to shake. Anything to hide the misery of the atmosphere in the room. Nobody knew what to say, and soon, person by person, the room emptied as her visitors, unable to cope with the events that had transpired, left the atmosphere of sadness and dismay and fled into the night, glad to be away from that miserable place and the long faces. Definitely not the social occasion of the year and an evening which was to forever leave her with a dislike of partying crowds and false bonhomie. She would never forget that day.

Emily took to her bed. Suzanne tactfully cleared up the mess and debris. She got rid of the empty bottles, washed and put away the dirty plates and cleaned the room. Her friend, the next day, would see no physical trace of what had transpired the previous evening. Just the hurt and pain would remain. How long would those linger on?

It was over. How to progress? Emily shuts her mind off everything around her. She could barely deal with the present, let alone the future. The phone stayed silent all day, their friends not knowing how to handle this delicate situation so they took the easy option. They felt for Emily, shocked by the crass behaviour of someone they had come to like and considered part of Emily's life into the future. Keep quiet and let the dust settle, they must have thought. Emily herself stayed in her bedroom all day, and Suzanne kept a low profile, tactfully leaving snacks and hot drinks just inside the door so that her friend could choose to notice them or not, as she felt fit.

Suzanne was unsure how to deal with what was happening. She had had a series of boyfriends but had never become serious with any of them. 'Mr Right' was still to put in an appearance and so she had never herself experienced such a situation. They were both so young, and this really was the first major blow they had faced in their lives. Until now, life had been free of drama. Their existence had been circumscribed by ease and support. Yes, they had complained and moaned about their existence. Small events had seemed significant and important but now Suzanne could understand that really what they had considered vitally important had been minor and lacking in magnitude. Not only Emily had to find a way forward, but so did her flatmate. They would both have to deal with the fallout.

Suzanne was a very different personality from her friend. Brought up in similar circumstances to Emily, she had, however, learned to approach life in a very dissimilar fashion. It had been of no importance to her that she would not be given the opportunity to study further after leaving school. Not academic, she was perfectly happy with that knowledge. Anxiety and angst were not part of her make-up, leaving her self-confident and content to make her way up the corporate ladder in an office environment. She also was not looking for any long-term romantic association at this stage in her life. Seeing the problems besetting Emily made her even more determined to play the field. London was heaving with eligible young men, and she was having great fun working her way through them one by one. Life was never perfect, she was discovering, but she could certainly take advantage of what London had to offer her; just shrug her shoulders with the annoying bits and go with the flow, she thought to herself. Grateful now for her current position and attitude to life, she listened to her friend's muffled sobs emanating from the neighbouring bed.

Emily, for her part, pulled the blankets over her head to stifle the sound of her crying. She didn't want Suzanne to hear but knew her friend could not help but be aware of her distress as she was sleeping in the same room. The future, which seemed so assured and enticing, had now disappeared in a flurry of words written in black ink on cream paper. She considered the saying that words can never harm you. Who had dreamed up such a nonsensical saying? The words on the sheets of paper would be etched onto her mind forever, she thought. They swirled around her brain like black demons with sharp, pointed barbs thrusting into her subconscious. Had Marcus actually considered how his words would impact her? Had he thought that he was being kind in his choice of phrases? She had never thought of him as cruel, yet some of the sentences which belittled her and her family were vicious and totally unnecessary. Was he just parroting his father, or was this what he truly believed? She had thought him essentially kind and considerate, loving her and wanting to stand by her and spend his life with her. How mistaken can you be, and how can you get things so wrong? She had totally misjudged him. And how could she trust anyone in the future after this fiasco? Now she discovered her judgement was obviously questionable, or she would have anticipated his terrible behaviour and lack of backbone in his clash with his parents. His parents considered her and her family 'not good enough' for their precious son. Apparently, he deserved better.

This was a body blow of unprecedented proportions. Her long relationship with Marcus had done so much to build up and consolidate her self-esteem, which had been of such a low calibre prior to meeting him. Now, she had to re-assess her whole entity, her abilities and her skill to make strong, sensible and reliable choices. Her brain was tied up in knots, unable to form a rational decision or see a way forward, and she had lost all confidence in herself, which had taken so long to develop and grow. It was smashed to pieces.

This man had seemed to be the whole, real deal. How wrong can you be? This was the dilemma which swirled around in her mind and to which she could find no answer or resolution. She was back to where she had been two years previously, just one among millions with no direction and no faith in herself. She had definitely not only lost a boyfriend but a large section of her essential being. Emily had obviously made a huge mistake, and now she had to search for a way to climb out of this mess and move forward in a positive fashion. This would not be easy, and she certainly was unable to deal with it at the time. She buried her head under a pillow and finally slept.

CHAPTER 6

Today was day one of the rest of her life.

Weeks had passed in a haze of routine and emptiness. Emily continued with her day-to-day existence, and each day passed in a blur of busyness and nothingness. Her social life had ground to virtually a complete halt, and her evenings were spent with a book or watching mindless television. The phone remained silent as her friends gave her space and time to reorientate. She did sometimes meet up with the odd friend and went for coffee or a meal out, but she knew she was not good company and did not blame them for keeping their distance. She kept thinking of ways to move forward and ramped up her desire to study for a degree, which would at least give her mind something to latch on to. By making enquiries, she convinced herself that she was being proactive and positive and not wallowing in self-pity.

Time, they say, is the great healer. Maybe it was a cliché, trotted out on so many occasions just to cover a multitude of scenarios. Walking down the busy street on her way to work one Monday morning, Emily suddenly felt a warm feeling course through her body. She looked around her as though seeing the world for the first time, at the many people intent on hurrying to their jobs, the light filtering thinly through the canopy of the trees, dappling the pavement with pools of light dancing in the light breeze. Suddenly, she understood that life and living were certainly definite options. For months, she had looked but not seen. Now, the film of pessimism was lifted from her eyes, and joy flooded into her limbs and heart, a glorious sensation. She was going to pull away from the all-enveloping cloak of negativity. She was going to take back control of her future. It was a eureka moment.

She had had a lucky escape. Marcus had not been the right man for her; that was obvious. If he had truly loved her, he would have fought her corner, not just dumped her ignominiously at such a seminal moment in her life. This certainly showed his selfishness and lack of awareness of how to treat a girlfriend, and it did not bode well for a future together. He was not worth agonising over. It was time to move on. What a relief!

How to deal with it? That was the big question. She certainly would not be defined by a relationship, by a man. She was her own person, a being in her own right with integrity, ability and personality, bright and intelligent, and she would not let him control her life for her, whether by his presence or now by his absence. This was a wholly new concept and one she would have to think about very carefully. Never in her life had she realised that she would ever think along these lines. She had spent her entire existence reacting to what life had thrown at her. Emily had just done what she had been told to do and lived her life according to the beliefs and desires of other people. A relationship followed by marriage was a given at that time. There was no alternative. As a woman, you were defined by your marital status and lacking a ring on your finger; you were destined for loneliness and misery. This was the course set out for her without her even realising it. She had never tried to set the agenda for herself, let alone set out her own path in life, so how was she going to do this now? She did not even know where to start to establish this new route for herself. This would need some considerable thought. She strode forward, her brain full to bursting with all these new concepts.

The day at work was, luckily, without problem or incident, just as well because her mind was constantly returning to her new-found philosophy. This would need to be developed and nurtured and a plan of campaign micro-managed. Steps would have to be taken to lead her to her newfound goal of self-sufficiency and independence.

Would she be strong enough to achieve these aims? Emily certainly hoped so.

Over their shared dinner that evening, Emily confided in Suzanne.

"I don't know what happened today, but something certainly did, miraculously. I was walking to work, and suddenly, it was like a floodlight had been switched on. I realised that Marcus was the past, just a blip in my existence, and there is life beyond. I've been thinking all day about what I'm going to do with my life, and I'm not going to waste any more time obsessing over that loser. Listen to what I've decided." She proceeded to tell Suzanne her thoughts and plans for the immediate future; a future free from angst and certainly free from pining over what can't be. Suzanne was delighted to see the return of hope and life in her lovely friend, but she still looked rather sceptical at the about-change and its apparent suddenness.

"I'm so happy to see this change in you. It's been horrible watching you since the fiasco of your birthday. I really do hope that you have found the answer and a way forward," she said.

"I must have been horrible to live with and you've been so patient with me. I really appreciate what you've done for me. Your friendship has been a godsend and I will never forget how you've been to me," Emily replied. "I know it isn't going to be easy, but I think, if I take things slowly, issues will pan out," she continued. "My first step is going to be to apply for that course I was interested in. Then, hopefully, if I'm accepted, I can feel my way from there. I'll meet all new people and be in a totally fresh environment. I was drowning in a swamp which was devouring me. Now, I'm emerging and pulling free. I'm getting excited just thinking about it."

Suzanne could see the gleam of hope shining out of her eyes. Her skin was flushed with colour, which had been totally lacking recently. It was wonderful to watch, and she prayed that it would all work out. She would give Emily her support but knew that she still lacked self-confidence, and this would maybe be just a moment of positivity and may not come to anything once the adrenaline of the initial excitement had worn off. Emily's essential vulnerability was a real problem lying just below the surface which would have to be faced. She could only wish for a positive outcome but could not be certain of that happening.

She didn't want to waste any time. The future beckoned enticingly, so the following morning, Emily took advantage of a day off work to go to the library to check out the course she was interested in and find out how to apply. She knew the form was a long one and it was important that she get it right. The librarian was helpful and pointed her in the right direction, wishing her luck in her application. It would be impossible to do a full-time course, so her best option would be to try and win a place at Birkbeck College, which had been established to help out people just like her who could only study in the evenings. This would allow her to continue her job at the same time. History was her favourite option, maybe with a teaching qualification as part of it, which would lead to a career. Teaching at the secondary school level or even to adults had always been a dream for Emily. It's definitely not teaching at a primary school as her headmistress had suggested. Now was her chance.

The form was as complicated as she had envisaged. In fact, it was a real nightmare. Emily made several copies to allow for mistakes but finally decided that she had completed it properly with no spelling mistakes or crossings. It had taken up the whole day, puzzling how to fill the answer boxes to show herself in the best and most positive light. She signed it in the space provided, put it in an envelope, stuck a stamp on it, walked to the nearest post box, and popped it through the slot. It was done! She now just had to await developments.

The waiting was truly awful. Every day, she rushed to the front door to see if a letter had arrived from the university. It was so stressful trying to concentrate on her work. She certainly could not afford to lose her job because she was not on the ball. Several weeks went by, but the day finally arrived when a big brown envelope plopped onto the mat. She sat at the table, Suzanne watching, barely daring to open it.

"For Pete's sake, Emily, just open it. Looking at it won't give you the answer! Do you want me to do the deed?"

"Absolutely not. Just give me a moment. I'm just so scared."

Emily ripped open the letter and glanced at the magic words, "We are pleased to inform you…." And let out a yelp of joy. She had an interview scheduled for the following week at the college at 7.30 pm. She jumped out of the chair, danced around the table, waving the letter in the air, grabbed hold of Suzanne in a bear hug and then collapsed back into her chair with a huge smile on her face. Stage one was complete. Now for stage two, the interview.

The next few days went by in a blur of excitement. She couldn't stop grinning and even occasionally laughed out loud. People glanced at her as they passed her in the street, and they smiled at seeing such an exultant young woman. Happiness is definitely contagious.

There were some preparations to make. She would need to find her certificates from her school days. Emily was pretty certain her mother had filed those away, so she would have to go to the house and collect them. She also needed to take some passport-size photos of herself with her for the interview. She hoped they would be more flattering than the usual horrendous official pictures she had had done in the past. Emily liked to look her best, even if it was only in official photographs. Decisions had to be made about what to wear and what time to leave to find her way to the college site in Bloomsbury. She did so, hoping that the interview would be a success and she could realise such a big dream. This could be life-changing.

Much to her surprise, the days sped by, and the big morning arrived. She had to go to work, but she couldn't imagine how she would manage all she had to do and sound intelligent and efficient when her mind was completely elsewhere. Despite her nervousness, she managed to survive the day, although keeping silent and not shouting her news from the rooftop had been incredibly difficult. She rushed home at the end of the day to change and get ready. She definitely wanted to make a good impression on every front.

The interview went well, beyond her expectations. The lecturer who spoke to her was warm and welcoming and told Emily that she thought she would be an asset to the college. The new potential students were given a tour of the building, its lecture halls, cafeteria and library by a young administrative assistant called Seth, who was cheerful and friendly, cracked jokes and generally put them all at ease. Emily came out of the building with a positive glow, though she knew she would have to wait for written confirmation of acceptance to the course.

The wait was not long this time, though it seemed endless. She was relieved and delighted when just a few days later, she was sent a confirmation letter of her acceptance on the course and left behind any niggling notion that she might be refused a place. She and Suzanne celebrated with an expensive meal and a good bottle of wine, and she rang her family and friends to tell them about her good fortune. Her parents were surprised at this new turn in her life but supportive, appreciating that their daughter needed to move on and find a new direction. The new term would start in October, and her life would move on a new trajectory.

CHAPTER 7

The first couple of weeks were a whirlwind of adjustment. Information, introductions, and timetables were thrown at the new students, and Emily quickly realised that she was not the only one on the course who seemed horribly overwhelmed. The students were a really mixed bunch from all ages and backgrounds, but they all had one thing in common: the desire to succeed. As Birkbeck only had lectures in the evenings, the days were still devoted to her day job, so it was necessary to pay the bills. She would only be attending college one evening a week, but she would need to find time to study and spend long hours in the library. She could see any potential social life fast disappearing over the horizon, but after the Marcus fiasco, this was no great loss. It would all be worth it in the end when she could wave her degree scroll, finally escape from the hated office and embark on a new career.

The library was a large building, several stories high, with tall stacks of books, study desks and places just to chill out and read. All Emily's research would have to take place here, so it was vital to find her way round the facilities so she could gain the most out of what it had to offer. To this end, the library employees held a series of tours to explain to the students how to access information, whether it be from books or newspaper cuttings. Her tour was conducted by Seth, the young man she had previously met. He was thorough and comprehensive with his information, joked with the students, and put them at ease. It was a revelation of how much there was to absorb and how much time it would take to get the hang of it all.

The cafeteria was maybe even more important. Here, the students met to discuss any issues they may have and to get to know each other. The student bar also had to be investigated! The drinks there were cheap and plentiful, and they all looked forward to spending many hours in those four walls. Most of the students were similar in age to Emily, but they ranged right up to people in their seventies who had never previously had the time or opportunity to follow their dreams and go to university. The wide array of people made the experience much more interesting, and people of all ages quickly found plenty in common and started to forge links and friendships. This was going to be fun.

Lectures started immediately. The first module was really an introduction with long reading lists and an explanation of what was required of the students. They all were apprehensive of the sheer volume of work that would be necessary, with constant essays having to be handed in, which had to be frighteningly long and of a high standard to justify good marks. The research needed was daunting, and a large proportion of the chatter in the cafeteria was on how to get their heads round this deluge of work. Furthermore, they had to maintain a standard in their day jobs if they were not to be sacked. Bills still had to be paid.

Emily made tentative new friendships with some of the students close to her own age but also with a slightly older woman, maybe in her forties, called Daisy. Daisy's parents, similarly to Emily's, had considered that university was not for the likes of her. After all, she was only going to get married and have children! This forged a bond between the young girl and the older woman, and they quickly found a routine of searching for each other and spending time together. They sat side by side in lectures and finished each evening with a drink in the bar, where they exchanged ideas and thoughts about the work they had to do.

Daisy, who was married with a couple of children, watched with interest as some of the young men circled round her young, attractive new friend and ran a running commentary on what she thought these fellows had in mind with regard to Emily. Emily, in turn, just laughed.

"I'm really not interested in any of them. I'm certainly not looking for any kind of relationship. I've had enough of that for the time being. Anyway, look at you. I know you love your husband, but why should you have to battle to achieve a life out of the house? There's more to living than washing up, cooking meals and scrubbing bathrooms. I don't think I want any of that."

"Oh, I don't know. There are benefits, though, and I agree I shouldn't have to fight my corner continuously. But look at that one over there. He looks really fun, and he's certainly very good-looking, and you should have some down time between studying and working."

"Forget it," Emily said dismissively. "I'm here to study, not get involved with any bloke. I've had all that in the past, but I certainly don't want to go down that route again. I just want to get stuck into the work here and make writing successful essays my number one priority."

"We'll see about that," her friend replied. Daisy was determined and intended to make it her mission to brighten up Emily's life with a love interest. Emily had told her all about her broken relationship, but despite all her denials that she was not prepared to meet up with any man, Daisy had other ideas about her new friend.

As the term progressed, modules were chosen from the options given, the first essay title was handed out, and its due date was given for handing in. Emily quickly established a routine of going straight from work to the library to do her research, spending several hours there each time sourcing books and taking notes. The librarian, Seth, soon made himself indispensable in this regard. Some books she could take home, but others were not permitted to leave the premises, so she sat at one of the desks, filling her notebook with her jottings from relevant material. Seth would carry the heavy volumes over to her desk, which really was not necessary, but he insisted. He certainly was charming and considerate, but he never hinted in any way that he was interested in her, which somewhat intrigued her. Most young men could not help themselves but say something flirtatious or what they considered clever or amusing. This made a very pleasant change.

Much to her relief, her first essay achieved a pass mark, certainly not brilliant, but she learned a great deal from the marker's comments in the margins. This was going to be a steep learning curve, and Emily was very clear in her mind that the next essay would achieve a higher passing grade. Daisy did better, and it was a conundrum for Emily, as her friend found time to do all the work, run a home, and take care of her family. Daisy's husband was old school and could not seem to understand that his wife might not be around to wait on him hand and foot. Like many men of his generation, he expected his dinner on the table when he arrived home from work, having earned the wherewithal to pay the bills and a nicely ironed shirt ready in his wardrobe for the next day. Daisy told her that she was training her children to be more independent and help around the house more. It was an uphill struggle, but she was determined that her son and daughter would have different perceptions of the roles of a man and a woman in society and within a marriage. Emily certainly agreed with this outlook. She, too, came from a family where the roles of the sexes were clearly defined, all in favour of the men in the household. After all, hadn't they moved on from the Victorian era? Sometimes, it did not seem so in the slightest. The sixties, with its vast societal changes, may have come and were going fast, but in too many ways, stultification remained all too present.

It was not easy. Emily would arrive home late at night after the weekly lectures and tutorials, longing to collapse into bed with a trashy novel, but she knew she had to start looking at her notes and start writing the next essay, the deadline of which was looming. There was little time for socialising, but she was determined to grab the odd coffee or meal with Suzanne or one of her friends. It would be all too easy to become obsessed with the workload, but she definitely did not want to lose out on her friendships, which were so vital to her. There was also her family to visit. In theory, they supported her decision to study but thought it was probably a waste of time. Her old-fashioned father told her one day that 'she was on the shelf' because she was now twenty-two and no man would be interested in her! Emily said nothing in reply but was totally shocked at how he seemed to deny the advances that women had made in the last couple of decades and, that emancipation was now a reality and that he had dismissed her marital expectations so easily and with such finality. His mindset was totally blinkered and out of step with the changing world which surrounded him. Unfortunately, he was not alone in his outlook.

A second term shot by with a speed that was terrifying. Another essay was handed in on a topic which interested Emily more than the previous one. This resulted in a higher mark, which was very satisfying and taught her that a deeper interest in a subject would certainly increase her game as she was more emotionally and intellectually engaged. She and Daisy, plus a few others, decided to hold a celebration in the college bar in order to mark the occasion of a job well done.

Emily and her friend took care of their outfits, hair and make-up. Emily was in a leather-look mini skirt with a loose, blue top over and made glitzy with silver chains and an abundance of bangles on her wrists. She loved fashion and adored dressing up and following the current trends, and now she definitely looked the part. Daisy grabbed hold of Emily's hand.

"Come on. Let's do this. You and I have some catching up to do in the drinking department," she shouted over the racket surrounding them. Emily smiled in agreement, and the two women pushed their way into the noisy, heaving bar, forcing their way to the front, where they met up with their friends. Drinks were ordered and downed, and bags of crisps were consumed as the music and the chatter increased in volume. Daisy left soon as she had to return home to her family. Her husband was not enthusiastic about the new direction in his wife's life but had to concede because she had made it quite clear that she was going on the course whatever he thought. Drink followed drink, and Emily realised that she was definitely somewhat high on booze and excitement. Her cheeks were flushed, her eyes brilliant, and her hair came loose from its band to flow round her shoulders. Someone put their hand on her shoulder and whispered something in her ear, which she could not make out due to the racket. She turned to see who it was. It was Seth.

He looked good. His dark hair contrasted with blue eyes, Irish colouring, but Emily knew he was all English. He was casually dressed in jeans and a t-shirt with a slogan emblazoned across the front, and he, too, had a drink in his hand as he leaned into her shoulder.

"You need someone to protect you in this chaos. You look so gorgeous somebody might kidnap you to have his wicked way with you."

Emily laughed at this ridiculous idea.

"As chat-up lines go, that must be the most pathetic I've heard in a long time, but I rather like the notion of a knight in shining armour coming to my rescue. Though I don't think there's much danger of that happening, do you?"

"Oh! There's an awful lot of evil people around ready to do just that" was his rejoinder. He gently pulled her away from the bar and managed to squeeze his way through the throng of people, lightly pulling Emily by the hand after him.

"It's boiling in there. Let's go outside and cool off. We can maybe go get a coffee to counteract all that alcohol. If you want to?" he said.

Emily nodded agreement, and they went downstairs, which led to a street of cafes and shops, mainly now shut for the night, but a couple remained open, and they ducked inside and found a table tucked away in a corner. Both ordered coffee and decided to share a cake. They were so deep in conversation that they barely noticed when their order was put in front of them. Seth was making her laugh with stories of students and their antics. He also recounted all the problems in running such a large library with irresponsible students and their equally irresponsible lecturers who so often refused to acknowledge rules and regulations and caused such a mess for the librarians to sort out. They chatted about their tastes in music, books, theatre, and a host of other areas, and the time sped by without their realising it.

The café staff started to give out strong intimations that it was really time to close up, and Emily and Seth took the hint when they started upending chairs onto the tables, and they walked outside into the cold night air. "I think they're trying to send us a message here, don't you think?" Seth said, taking her hand as he walked her to the station, giving her a light, quick kiss on the cheek and leaving her by the entrance to the tube.

The train arrived, and she only had to go to a few stops, which did not give Emily much time to assess this new situation. She had not been out with anyone since her breakup with Marcus, and she really had to consider whether she was in the right frame of mind to start a new relationship. Of course, she might be jumping the gun here. Maybe Seth just looked upon her as a pleasant companion for an inebriated evening. Or maybe he already had a girlfriend or even a fiancée. He had told her he was not married. What did she actually want? This was all very confusing, and her mind was a total jumble of half-baked thoughts and ideas.

She had to admit that she had had more fun that evening than in a long time, and it gave her a warm fuzzy feeling of being appreciated. It was good for her ego that somebody found her attractive and good company. Or maybe his attraction to her was all in her imagination. She really needed to work on her self-confidence and have more faith in herself. Emily knew that this was a perennial problem for her. For the moment, she was really far too tired to work it out, and she didn't want to miss her stop. She would spend time with Suzanne tomorrow and talk it through with her. Her friend would see what was happening from a different viewpoint, and it would help clarify her thoughts. For now, she just let the warmth of her feelings wrap her in a cloak of happiness and excitement waiting to come.

The following day, she spent the entire time at work dealing with routine and somewhat dull administration. Emily really disliked office work and looked forward to having a qualification tucked under her belt, which would finally liberate her from this treadmill, which was so monotonous to her. But her degree course was three years, and she had hardly started, so it would be some considerable time before she could escape. She would just have to grin and bear it and count down the days to her release from this tedium.

Thursday evening was her college evening. She wanted to arrive early so she could reach the library with plenty of time to do some research for her next essay and maybe catch sight of Seth. She was in two minds about whether she wanted something to come of this connection and thought seeing him again might help make the decision for her.

Emily swung through the doors into the library and looked over at the reception desk. No-one was there. She felt a frisson of disappointment but went to the stacks to find the books she needed and sat herself down at an empty desk to start on her work. Time passed quickly, and suddenly, she felt a hand on her shoulder. There was Seth, with his blue eyes and dark wavy hair, and she realised that she was thrilled at the touch of his heavy hand on her sweater.

"What time do your lectures finish tonight? Would you meet me afterwards for a coffee? I've really missed you," he said quietly into her ear.

"I'll see you at the café on the corner," Emily replied, trying to appear cool and slightly detached, though in reality she was anything but. Seth nodded and moved away. Emily turned back to her books but with an intense feeling of excitement and anticipation. Was this the start of something new, or would it just fizzle out quickly? She had no idea but certainly wanted to find out. She really couldn't think about it for now. She had work to do.

Emily attended the lectures and updated Daisy on what was happening later. Her friend was so pleased for her and delighted that Emily was maybe on the cusp of something big, but it was still in the early days. The two friends parted company, and Emily went out of the big building and found Seth already seated in the café. He certainly was a charmer and had the gift of the gab, even if he was not Irish. Maybe he had visited Ireland and kissed the Blarney Stone? They talked about their plans for the future. Emily told him about her desire to teach in a secondary school.

"I like working in the library, and I think it would be a good long-term career choice. I would need to take some courses in library studies, which would be somewhat problematic. Maybe I can study and work at the same time, the way you are. I would have to investigate what options are available," he explained. He had never been to university, which was an issue, but one that could be overcome, he told her.

He was maybe three years older than her, she calculated. People eddied around them, coming and going, but they seemed totally unaware of their surroundings as they concentrated on each other. It seemed magical to Emily. She was feeling more and more attracted to Seth. He was so attentive, anticipating her every wish, and she started to feel very secure in his company.

"Oh my goodness. I didn't realise how late it was. I mustn't miss the last train. Will you walk me to the station, please?" Seth took her hand in his as they walked side by side. He said goodbye at the entrance to the station with a kiss on the cheek. He was certainly not rushing things, which Emily found very comforting as she hated to be pressured into a relationship. She was still hurting from Marcus's betrayal and the pain it had caused her. She now wanted to take things slowly and let things develop gradually and carefully.

They fell into a routine, seeking each other out on a Thursday. Seth could certainly talk! He was amusing and articulate and never made a move that made her nervous. He took his time, putting her at her ease, listening to her and her dreams. Emily told him about her relationship with Marcus and how badly she had been hurt, which made her anxious about throwing herself into any new liaison. She needed time to heal. Seth seemed to understand and held back from forcing her to make decisions.

He told her that he had left school with no qualifications. His parents did not seem to care about his education and demanded that he find a job and help support the family finances. Seth was obviously very bright, and it seemed tragic that he had not been encouraged to find his role in life. He had found a part-time job in the local library as a helper but now was trying to work his way upward. Despite having told her he would need more qualifications, he did not seem to be doing much to make this happen. This surprised Emily and, if truth be told, somewhat shocked her that someone so able was just letting matters drift to such an extent. She attempted to motivate him, and he agreed with her and promised he would be more proactive.

Walking to the station hand in hand, Seth asked Emily if she would go out with him for dinner on the coming Saturday night.

"I think that's a lovely idea," Emily quickly replied. "Where do you think we should go? There's that new Italian restaurant. It's supposed to be great. I know several people who have said the food is lovely and really recommend it. Shall we try there?" This relationship was taking a new turn, and Emily hoped she would not regret it. She had to jump in feet first and hope that all would be well. Sometimes, you just have to take a chance in life, she thought. She had high hopes.

CHAPTER 8

Emily had to admit that she was smitten. Dinner with Seth had been everything she had dreamed of. The Italian restaurant was a small, family-run affair that was so fashionable at that moment, right down to the raffia-bound Chianti bottles holding candles that had dripped wax down the sides. They ordered pasta for Emily and a huge pizza for Seth, the size of a cartwheel, which made them giggle at the outlandish enormity of it. The wine flowed, and the food kept coming. They ate off each other's plates and shared desserts, feeding each other using the same fork while gazing at each other with slightly inebriated eyes.

"What do you want from life?" he asked her after licking clean the last of the tiramisu from the fork.

Emily thought for a moment about this question that nobody had ever asked her before.

"To be happy," she said. "That's the most important thing. Everything else is of secondary importance. I just have to find a way to get to that stage. It's like playing with a number of balls, throwing them up in the air and trying to balance them so that they make a pattern. If I find the secret to how to do that, then I think happiness will follow. It's understanding what elements are necessary to achieve this. That's what I'm trying to discover. And the right person to share it with."

Was Seth the right person, she mused to herself. His background and upbringing were very different from hers. His family, while certainly not poverty-stricken, were nevertheless from a somewhat impoverished environment. His mother was a helper in a school, and his father worked as a clerk for the local council. Seth said little about his parents, and she wondered about the family dynamics. He seemed so straightforward and uncomplicated but was reticent about his own experiences on the home front. This didn't worry her unduly, and she felt that she could trust him, tell him anything. He always gave her his full attention and remembered every detail of previous conversations. Emily knew that she was somewhat naïve, having been brought up in a family where there were no real problems. Both her parents had grown up in households where money was greatly lacking but had worked hard, found success, and now wanted their children to continue to live a similar lifestyle. Her parents rarely disagreed in front of her, and she had no experience of the seamier side of life. She knew it existed. After all, she did read the papers, but it was difficult to appreciate the reality of lives lived under the umbrella of criminality, poverty or violence. Her world was one of security, comfort and love, free from stress of any meaningful gravity. Obviously, there had been issues, but there were no great consequences. She was loved and cherished by her parents. She now felt safe with Seth even if his upbringing had been so different from her own. He was kind and thoughtful, and she considered that she could distinguish in him a safe pair of hands.

Emily let herself into her flat and found Suzanne sitting on the sofa, having just returned herself from an evening with a new boyfriend. She was playing the field. She agreed but was unrepentant. Plenty of time to settle down was her motto, and Emily sometimes wondered how her friend could remember all their names. They came and went so fast! They updated each other, comparing notes and laughing at some of the issues that had arisen on their dates. They then settled in to discuss the new turns of events, dissected them, and chuckled at the ironies and frustrations that seemed to be part and parcel of dating. Emily talked at length about her feelings and reactions to her new boyfriend, and she found that articulating out loud with her friend helped to clarify her mind and perceptions about this very new relationship. It was still early days, and she certainly was not going to rush matters. Suzanne also agreed with her that she should take her time and make very sure of her feelings before committing herself irrevocably. Their respective love lives differed wildly, but each appreciated the other and celebrated their individuality. They chatted on late into the night, pleased with how their lives were panning out and how, for once, everything seemed to be moving smoothly.

The weeks seemed to fly by. Libraries were visited regularly, lectures attended, essays written and handed in, all organised round her day job and regular meetings with Seth and making new friendships. Seth would bring round bagels and smoked salmon on a Sunday morning, which he knew she loved, and Suzanne would join them in the living room, eating off their laps with the weekend papers strewn around their feet. Although a routine had become established, nevertheless, Seth always managed to find something fun to do. They loved to go clubbing to one of the many discos that had sprung up recently, and they would dance the night away to the throbbing beat of the latest pop sounds and sing along when they knew the words. Theatres were visited, seated in the gods, and regular outings to the cinema. Eating out was rare as money was a problem, and so Emily would cook something simple at home. The time had come for her to present the new man in her life to her family, and this was arranged for the following weekend. She was confident that her parents would love her new boyfriend, and she was excited to introduce him and obtain their approval. It would be lunch on Saturday.

"It's really scary meeting the family for the first time", Seth demurred. "What if they hate me? They must be worried after how your last relationship ended."

"Just be yourself. I'm sure they'll love you just as much as I do, and we really have to get it over and done with it. And I'm also really worried about meeting your parents. The apprehension works both ways, and we just have to deal with this stage in our relationship," Emily replied.

"You're right, I suppose. We just need to dive in and get on with it."

The day had come, and the two young people set off bearing flowers and chocolates on the train out to the suburbs and the long-awaited meeting. Seth had taken some effort with his outfit, Emily noted. He had gone for a smart though casual look with none of the current fashion excesses which might frighten her parents off. She really wanted him to make a good impression. Her family's reaction and approval were so important to her. What would she do if they hated him? She was definitely anxious but tried to hide her nervousness from Seth.

The moment had come. Her mother opened the door and hugged her daughter, and Emily quickly introduced Seth, who shook hands with both parents.

"Come in, it's lovely to meet you at last," Emily's mother said.

"I've heard so much about you from Emily that I couldn't wait to finally meet you. Now I see who Emily gets her good looks from. You're so alike," Seth answered.

"Well, the apple never falls far from the tree, and that's certainly true of my wife and daughter. Compliments to my wife though will take you far, though I have to admit I always thought Emily took after me more," her father joked. He showed the two young people into the house.

"You have a gorgeous home. It's so stylish yet warm and friendly. I would love somewhere like this one day," Seth answered.

Flowers and chocolates were handed over and admired, and her mother went to put the flowers in water while Emily's dad offered them a drink. Niceties dealt with it, they all went to sit in the living room, with drinks in hand and nibbles handed around. Seth was gazing around him, taking in the décor, the pictures, and the beautiful old fireplace with its logs, which emitted warmth throughout the room. A fire guard protected them from sparks that might fly out, and the family cat was basked in a basket and carefully placed so it could get full benefit from its flames.

It was obvious, Emily noted, that her parents were as worried as she was about meeting her latest conquest, and they were very obviously trying not to ask too many personal questions so as not to seem intrusive. The conversation flowed quite nicely until they went to sit round the dining table to start on the lavish and gorgeous lunch her mother had prepared. Food was brought in on numerous platters, more than generous in its copious quantities and variety. Plates were piled high, and wine was poured into elegant crystal, followed by a choice of fabulous and exotic desserts. It was a veritable feast. Emily's mother must have worked so hard to produce all this gorgeous food.

The afternoon passed with no apparent awkwardness or difficult moments, or so it seemed to Emily, but she exhaled a huge sigh when it was time to leave, coats on and the door shut closed behind them. I really had been quite an ordeal, she considered to herself.

“They seem nice. Just as you described them, but I really couldn’t get a feel of what they thought of me. Your mum looked at me sideways a couple of times as though she was trying to assess me. What was your view of their idea of me?”

“It’s difficult really to know” Emily answered. “It all seemed to go well, but after my experience with Marcus, they really are very protective of me. I’ll speak to my mother later, or maybe tomorrow and see what she has to say. I’m sure it will be all right.”

They sat in silence on the train back to Emily’s flat, both deep in their own thoughts while they each tried to work out how the lunch had gone. They would have to go through the whole process again with Seth’s parents, but he was not close to his family so, there was less pressure on that score. Seth really did not seem to care deeply about his parents’ reactions to his girlfriend, and, as far as he was concerned, it was just a formality to be gone through. This was a strange concept to Emily, whose ties to her family were deep and vitally important to her. She needed their validation. She and Seth spent the evening together, talking over how the day had gone. Now, she was on her own with her own thoughts. She would speak to her parents tomorrow.

Sure enough, the phone rang shortly before supper the next day. Emily quickly picked up the receiver, desperate to hear her mother's opinion of Seth. Who could fail to love him? He had so much going for him; he was good-looking, polite, charming, and fun. Surely her mother would agree?

"What did you think, Mum? Did you like him?"

There was a short silence, which worried Emily. What was wrong? Why didn't her mother answer straightaway?

"He certainly is everything you say, very persuasive and attractive," her mother finally said. "I can certainly understand what attracts you to him."

"I'm sorry, but I don't understand what you're saying. You make that sound like a criticism rather than a compliment. Is being charming a crime? He really is very thoughtful and considerate, which makes a great change from some I've met," Emily countered. This was definitely not going the way she had anticipated, and she could feel a veil of misery descending on top of her head like the beginning of a really nasty migraine.

"I've just found in the past that there is often a hidden agenda when somebody seems to be trying too hard. It makes me want to see what is being hidden if there is too much upfront. I think you should be careful and not rush into something. You seem to be moving very fast, and that worries me. Just please take your time," she replied.

Emily found herself getting angry at her mother, also hurt and bewildered. Her throat was seizing up, and it was difficult to get her voice to work, but she had to counter what her mother said and get to the bottom of all this. She thought that Seth had behaved impeccably, and she just couldn't understand her mother's apprehension. Her mother obviously sensed her daughter's frustration, but life had taught her that everything that seems perfect very often is far from being that. It was a difficult position to be in. On one hand, she didn't want to upset her daughter, but on the other hand, she wanted to warn her that her intuition was troubling her and that Emily should be very careful.

"I think that you have to meet his family and then decide where his background lies, what motivates him and what makes him tick. You have to dig deeper and take it from there. I don't want to discourage you, but I want you, more than anything, to build a good relationship and have happiness in your life. That is my main desire for you. Please, please take care."

Emily put down the phone, made herself a hot drink, and sat down to consider the conversation with her mother. She was still shaking from the impact of her mother's words and could not conceive why her mother had such doubts. Seth was always such a gentleman with her, anticipating her every desire and move, constantly supportive and loving. What was not to like? On the other hand, her parents were older and more experienced, and if they thought there was a problem, then she really should think the matter through and not discard it out of hand.

Backwards and forward went her mind. The more she questioned the issue, the more upset and angry she became with her parents. What did they know about Seth? They had only met him for a couple of hours, and it was impossible to pin down somebody's personality during such a brief meeting, wasn't it? She had spent so many hours and days with him, and surely she was more eligible to make a rational judgement? All her friends seemed to like him. Nobody had said anything adverse about him. But would they do so if they thought it would distress her? They would want to be tactful in what they said, but they all seemed to be happier when they were with him. He certainly was very good company and the heart of any gathering. Obviously, the next step would be to meet his family, she decided. She would tell Seth that this had to happen quickly. She would certainly not breathe a word to him of her parents' misgivings.

Seth had been hesitant about taking her to his parents' home, but she insisted. It would give her an insight into his background and upbringing, which would help her understand his life choices and what made him tick. He gave in, and they planned to call in a couple of days' time, not for a meal but just for a casual visit. It was obvious that he lacked enthusiasm, but it had to go through. His family could not just be ignored or sidelined.

They took the underground and walked the road to the council estate in which they lived. It was an inner-city area made up of high-rise blocks of flats and semi-detached and terraced houses probably built in the fifties. The streets were not too bad but could have done with more trees and green spaces. Graffiti was the main source of decoration for the walls, just tagging and rude comments, certainly nothing artistic. It was a far cry from the leafy suburbs where Emily had been brought up with their detached homes, generous gardens and expensive cars parked in the driveways.

Seth became more and more silent as they walked through the streets, navigating discarded cycles and empty bottles. They finally arrived at one of the houses, which appeared well-kept and tidy in comparison to some of its neighbours. They walked up the short path while Emily looked around her. The net curtains in the windows seemed clean, and the small front garden was neat if somewhat uninspiring. The family car was parked outside and, although old, was also newly washed. They rang the bell and waited. Seth's father opened the door, and he and his son shook hands. They had not seen each other in several months, but the two men assessed each other, looking each other up and down. Emily noted that there was a total lack of warmth.

"You look well," his father finally said. He turned to Emily, taking her hand and holding it for fractionally too long. "Welcome, it's good to meet a friend of Seth's. Please come in and meet my wife."

His wife came into the room. She was neat in her dress. Hair pulled back into a ponytail. Emily could now see who Seth looked like. He was the image of his mother except for the colour of his eyes, which he had inherited from his father. They all smiled at each other, but there was tension in the room. Seth and his parents saw each other very infrequently, and Emily wanted to discover and understand what was the root of this estrangement and the dynamics of their relationship. Immediately, his father took charge of the conversation. His mother sat silent and mute while his father dominated the room. He asked Emily a great number of questions about her life, home, education and career. It was more a cross-examination than a conversation. Seth did not interrupt and just listened with a sullen look on his face throughout.

Tea was offered and served with a shop-bought cake and biscuits. Seth's mother bustled around, keeping busy and out of the way of the conversation, occasionally glancing at her husband with disinterest as though she had heard it all before. The time passed awkwardly, and it was obvious Seth just wanted to get out of there, and Emily certainly felt likewise. They finally left the house and walked away in silence, each busy with their own thoughts, Emily felt the need to assimilate all that had transpired and then analyse her thoughts and try to come to some conclusions.

CHAPTER 9

Seth was sulking.

They had returned to Emily's flat with hardly a word between them, neither knowing where to begin. She was confused by the meeting with his parents, so different from her own. She couldn't think what to say to ease the situation. She had always taken her upbringing for granted. Certainly, it had not been perfect, but she had never realised until now how fortunate she had been in her life. Seeing the contrast between her loving family and his cold and disinterested one was a real shock to her. Seth was taciturn, angry, and resentful, having been put in the position of thrusting to the fore the difference between the two sets of parents and their lifestyle. They somehow had to break through this barrier and find mutual territory and a way to find the best in each other and create their own reality.

She tried to start a conversation, but Seth continued to sulk. Emily was seeing a new side to her boyfriend. Was he embarrassed? Maybe he felt inferior? Why should that be? His parents seemed decent enough people. Not everybody was a great success in life, making huge sums of money and living the lifestyle of which they had always dreamed. This did not make them inferior in any way. Certainly, Emily had not taken to Seth's father. She had found him overbearing and maybe something of a bully. His mother had been mainly silent and seemed used to her husband's behaviour. She had looked cowed and resigned to her husband's need to take charge and impose his personality on others.

Seth, too, had let his father's constant flow of words silence him. Emily could now see why he did not talk much about his upbringing, but she would not judge Seth by his parents. He was his own person and had broken out of the family fold to make his personal mark in life and steer his own path to a future in which he would be in control. They really needed to discuss the situation, but Seth refused to open up, and they parted in silence. Maybe a night's sleep would sort out the situation, and he would be more willing to engage then. They did, however, agree to meet after work for a meal out the following day.

Emily had a sleepless night, with her mind whirling with all sorts of thoughts, and she staggered into work in the morning with gritty eyes and a feeling of deep despondency. Her job was busy, however, and she managed to steer through the day by keeping occupied and engaged, but it finally came to an end. They were to meet up at a nearby restaurant where they would maybe have the chance to discuss the problems the visit had thrown up. As far as Emily was concerned, there were no difficulties, but Seth obviously felt otherwise.

He was sitting at the table when she walked in. He jumped up and gave her a big hug and a huge kiss, smiling and laughing. Emily was stunned and delighted. She had not expected this turnaround at all. He certainly was capable of surprising her. She decided not to mention the events of the previous day in any great detail, but they could not be totally ignored. He obviously had either put the whole matter behind him or had decided to disregard it. Either way, Emily was happy to go along with the bright and cheerful Seth she knew and loved. They picked up the menus the waiter had placed in front of them, studied them made their choices and waited for him to bring them their food.

“Well, you seem in a happier mood today” she said. “I wasn’t expecting this at all. You seemed so fed up and miserable yesterday.”

“There’s nothing to talk about. It is what it is, and we should just move on. I don’t want to discuss this any more and analyse deep psychological meanings or pull apart everything said or felt. It's a waste of time and energy. I just want to be with you and enjoy our time together."

Emily was somewhat taken aback by this somewhat defensive reply but decided not to continue, dropped the subject, and just was happy that Seth seemed to have come to terms with the situation, as it was. Maybe it was not such a big difficulty as she had thought. Maybe she was overthinking his behaviour. She would let it pass and enjoy the meal and the moment, just so relieved that things were back to normal. She felt so confident in the relationship and thought it had a wonderful future. Obviously, problems would arise, but they could be dealt with, couldn't they?

Nothing more was said. It was as though the visit to his parents had never happened. Seth continued his outgoing, cheerful self, so Emily decided that she would never allude to it again. She changed the subject to a lighter note, and the conversation returned to a repartee, which was infinitely easier to cope with.

They continued to meet several times a week, taking walks in the park and visitings to the cinema and theatre, which they both enjoyed. Hours were spent in companionable silence reading the newspapers or the latest novel. Emily continued with her studies and made good progress. Maybe she was not at the top of the class, but she managed to achieve creditable marks in the work she presented. Daisy, on the other hand, performed brilliantly. How did she manage it? All was well in her world, and she felt truly happy and blessed in her life and relationship.

One day, her mother phoned to say that she and her husband had rented a house in Bournemouth for a couple of weeks in order to take a well-earned break. "Would you and Seth like to join us for the weekend? There will be plenty of room for you to stay as the house is a good size and can accommodate a large number of people. It overlooks the sea, and there is plenty to do in the area besides going to the beach. The New Forest is close by, as is Poole, with its beautiful harbour and famous pottery. There will be sailing and swimming walks on the beach and a chance to gain knowledge of each other in an idyllic setting, so different from your usual environment."

"I'll have a word with Seth. I'm sure he'll love to come. It sounds wonderful," she replied. Sure enough, Seth was very enthusiastic about the idea of the break, and it was decided they would go down for the weekend in a couple of weeks' time.

They would take the last train down on the Friday as they both had to go to work, go home and get ready. It was not a long journey, so they booked return train tickets. Emily would go round to Seth's flat, and they would go together to the station. It would be their first journey together out of London. Emily hoped it would go well and started thinking of what to wear and what to pack. It really was exciting, and she could not wait for the day to come. Seth also seemed keen and talked about the places he would like to visit, especially the New Forest with its wild ponies.

The day finally came, and, after what seemed an endless day at work, Emily rushed home, collected her small suitcase and made her way round to Seth's to go together to Waterloo station. They would have about an hour and a half to reach the station, which was plenty of time, and they would not have to rush.

She arrived at Seth's place, and he opened the door for her.

"I just have to have a quick shower", he said.

"Don't be too long. There's no mad rush, but we can't hang around."

"Don't worry. We'll make it in plenty of time". He called from the bathroom. Time passed, and Seth did not appear.

Emily looked at her watch and saw it was later than she had realised. She went to the bathroom and banged on the door.

"Please hurry. It's getting really late, and if you are any longer, we'll miss the train," she shouted through the door.

"Don't get your knickers in a fucking twist. There's plenty of time," he shouted back.

Emily started to get very upset, especially by his very crude reply. What was that about? Never before had he used such language to her. She could not understand why he was taking so long. He finally appeared with a towel wrapped around his waist.

"I'll just get dressed. Won't be long" and disappeared into the bedroom.

"Please hurry, we're really cutting it very fine."

He finally appeared, but this left them hardly any time to get to the station. Emily almost shoved him out of the door, and they ran for the bus, which did not arrive for several minutes. They collapsed onto their seats, but Emily could tell that they would be very lucky to have made the train on time, and it was the last one of the evening. They arrived at the station, ran to the platform and watched as the train receded from the platform with a long blow of its horn. They had missed the train.

Emily was mortified, particularly as Seth did not seem particularly concerned. He just shrugged his shoulders as she berated him.

"So we'll get the first train in the morning," he said. "It's not important. What's the big deal? You worry too much about minor matters."

"But my parents are expecting us, and it's not a 'minor matter'. They'll be at the station to meet us, made arrangements for the evening. Why did you take so long when you knew we had a deadline to meet?" she almost shouted.

He shrugged his shoulders once again. Why was he being like this, she asked herself. It's almost as if he deliberately missed the train. That was a ridiculous idea, surely? Why would he do that? He was usually quite good at timekeeping, and this did not relate to her experiences with him. He seemed in no way sorry and unwilling to take responsibility for missing the train. It was this and a complete lack of guilt for his actions which so confused her. If she had been the cause of missing the train, she would have been mortified.

This time, it was her turn to sulk and be miserable. Seth behaved as if nothing had occurred as they made their way back to his flat to spend the night. He laughed and joked and tried to chivvy her out of her bad mood, but she would not cooperate. He seemed totally unaware of her feelings and still completely lacking in remorse, and there was absolutely no sign of an apology for his behaviour.

Emily had spoken to her parents and told them that they would come the following morning first thing. Her mother said little about what had occurred and was largely silent while Emily did most of the talking and apologising.

They arrived in Bournemouth mid-morning, and Seth greeted her parents like long-lost friends, joked, and complimented her mother on her outfit. He enthused the cottage with its glorious views over the limpid sea and worked hard to charm his way back into their good books. Emily relaxed as her parents seemed to accept their late arrival, and plans were made for the days ahead.

Her parents took Emily aside and told her of their dismay at their missing the train, and Emily had to be rather disingenuous about how it had occurred. She felt protective of Seth and was unwilling to face the fact that maybe he was not as perfect as she had thought. She was blinded by love and refused to see anything bad in her lover, nor could she envisage that he could be less than perfect.

The weekend stuttered to a close, goodbyes exchanged, and the young couple caught the train back to London with no further mishaps. Emily did not bring up the matter of the missed train, and Seth seemed to have shrugged off the incident without any further regret, explanation or apology.

Life settled back into its routine. Emily was nearing the end of her course and was preparing her final thesis, which had to be handed in before the end of the summer term. She was quietly confident that she would achieve a satisfactory grade, although she knew she was not one of the high-flyers. She had accepted that reality long ago and was happy with the knowledge that she had done her best throughout her time at university. With the end of term fast approaching, they planned a few days away together in Scotland, which neither of them had ever visited but knew to be beautiful and historic, although notoriously plagued with bad weather. They would wait until nearer the time to see if the elements would be kind to them before making their final decision.

CHAPTER 10

Emily was almost sick with excitement. The thought of going on holiday with Seth for the very first time filled her with hope and a tinge of apprehension. She did not count the weekend with her parents as a true holiday, and now she would be spending a week alone with her boyfriend with no outside interference. It would be just the two of them, a chance to discover a deeper relationship and understand the nuances of their personalities and how they gelled together. It would give her a chance to look deeply into what made him the person he appeared on the surface and an opportunity to learn if he was the 'one'. In her mind, she had, for quite a while now decided that this was the individual she wanted to spend her life with. His charm, thoughtfulness, and care for her were aphrodisiacs for her well-being, and he did much to raise her levels of self-confidence.

Their backgrounds, certainly, could not be more dissimilar. His upbringing in a household with little luxury contrasted deeply with her own. There was also the question of their differing educational attainments. Emily had stayed at school until the age of 18, collecting a plethora of good exam results and qualifications. She had now topped this off with a university degree. Seth, on the other hand, had been told to leave school at 16, the minimum age possible and was not given the opportunity to gain even the most basic qualifications. He had been told to earn a living and help contribute to the family coffers. He most certainly had the ability to study and succeed but had been denied the chance to do so. Emily was very conscious of how fortunate she had been in comparison. On the other hand, she had been much more proactive, not accepting the role in life her parents had subscribed for her but going out to make things happen. Hence, the degree and proper qualifications needed to advance in life. Seth had shown no sign of taking charge of his progression. Matters and life were just left to drift.

She saw that Seth wanted to improve himself. He read widely and enjoyed the same cultural activities as herself. He was articulate and literate, although she had to admit to herself that he did not seem to have the same strong work ethic that she possessed, nor did he seem to be proactive in finding ways of moving forward and upward. She considered that these were issues which could be dealt with in time, and their youth was a time to be spent enjoying the moment. That was what Seth told her, anyway. This was somewhat disquieting, but they had their whole future before them to iron out these problems. He always spoke with such certainty that she never questioned his reasoning.

They had decided to travel up to Glasgow by train and then hire a car there so that they could wander through the towns and countryside at their own pace without being restricted by timetables. They did not miss the train! It was the first time she had ever travelled the length of the country, and her excitement was palpable. Emily gazed out of the window at the changing scenery through the housing estates and industry on the outskirts of London and then northwards. By the Midlands, the green of the countryside was taking precedence, and she sat glued to the window, only occasionally chatting and passing remarks to Seth, who seemed correspondingly fixated on the landscape. The farms seemed so neat, and the fields were almost manicured in appearance, with sheep and cows keeping down the grass. The corn was almost ready to be harvested, and hopefully, the weather would stay dry so that the farmers could bring in the crops.

They collected the car near Glasgow's main station and drove past the smoke-blackened buildings of the town. The city was soon left behind, and they followed the narrow, twisting road, sharing the driving, heading towards the Trossachs and Loch Lomond, which was not too far of a journey. The scenery was breathtaking, and they were mesmerised by the combination of hills, water and picturesque houses surrounding the lochside. Small islands dotted the water, emerald green with their cover of trees. Pleasure craft of varying sizes bobbed in the water, and sailing boats cut across the loch, with ducks and other wildlife tottering in the wake of the waves. They rode out the currents which tossed them into the air, but they seemed confident in their ability to crest the miniature tidal wave. Close to the shore, more birds of diverse breeds scavenged for food, attracted by the tourists with their tempting sandwiches and other edible delights. They watched them in fascination, trying to name them but could only manage a handful. They obviously needed a quick, short introduction to recognise wildfowl. They would spend the night here and found the small hotel they had booked overlooking the water and a jetty. Dinner under the still-light sky at the edge of the water was romantic and totally sublime. The sun stayed high with a marvellous clear quality in the extended summer evening of this northern part of the country. All was well with Emily and her world, she thought. She would remember this her whole life as a time of sheer perfection.

Scotland was truly fabulous. The weather gods were smiling at them, obviously in tune with young lovers and set on bringing romance and a little bit of heaven into their lives. The scenery was stunning, and they were constantly turning a bend in the twisting roads, and a glorious new vista would open up to enchant the eye. The combination of hills, water, vistas and valleys seemed to merge into an idyll of loveliness, which was breathtaking and totally overwhelming in its perfection. They were truly blessed by the fine weather in this land, which is so famous for its gentle rains and mists that would descend and blot out the landscape in a flash. They moved westwards, then north up the coast through Oban. They splurged out on a ferry to the Isle of Mull and adored the quaint seaside village of Tobermory with its row of harbour cottages. Each painted a different pastel colour resembling a rainbow of prettiness. They continued further north up the coast, reaching the Kyles of Lochalsh and the ferry to Skye. There was talk about a connecting bridge, but that would be sometime in the future. Now, the lure of the ferry drew them on. The long summer evenings were a real bonus, and it never really grew completely dark. The only downside was the famous Scottish midges, which surrounded them in swarms of nastiness, but Emily had read about this scourge and had come prepared, loaded with masses of insect repellent. A night's stay in Skye was behind them, and they had landed up in the gorgeous lochside village of Plockton. They had their final dinner of local fish just caught that day by the local fishermen, accompanied by a good bottle of wine. The restaurant had laid their table on a jetty pushing out onto the water, the huge sky filled with stars only putting in an appearance very late as the night was held back by the sun dipping into the sea just for a short time this far north. The waters lapped the shores, and the dramatic hillsides on the far side of the loch provided a background to complete the perfection. Nothing could have been more romantic than sitting in such a paradise with your lover. It was definitely a truly idyllic ending to a wonderful week before they needed to return to the big city and the train down south to London and reality. Life was certainl" wonderful, mused Emily.

Dessert was finished, and they lingered at the table, chatting quietly. The talk turned to their futures and how they could combine their lifestyles. Before she knew it, they were talking about marriage. Emily could not think how the conversation had taken this turn. Which one of them had introduced it? Suddenly, they were talking about dates and locations, and Emily thought she was dreaming or hallucinating. They smiled at each other, both taken unaware by the turn the conversation had taken and strolled hand in hand back to the quayside inn where they were staying. Emily's mind took a long time to switch off as the churning thoughts kept colliding in her brain. They talked for hours, going through the various options, daydreaming their thoughts out loud and smiling at some of the ideas and thoughts which popped into their heads and suddenly were articulated. Sleep finally came, lying in each- other's arms and lulled by the gentle lap of the loch's waters washing onto the shore.

The long journey home was spent discussing plans for the future. Where to get married? Where to live? Would they have enough money to combine their salaries? What would be the reaction of family and friends? This was a particular angst to Emily as she was well aware that her parents had deep-seated doubts about Seth's suitability to marry their daughter. Would they oppose her in any way? There was certainly plenty to keep her agonising.

The train finally drew into the station, and the two young people separated to go to their respective homes. They had agreed to let their families know of their decision to marry early that evening, and they would meet up the following day. Emily could not wait to tell Suzanne her amazing news, and as soon as she heard her friend's key in the door, she rushed to hug her. Suzanne held her close and then pushed her gently back and gave her a long, hard look.

"Well, you certainly look like the cat that's swallowed the cream. Do tell. I gather it was a good trip, but from the look on your face, there's more going on, isn't there?" she said.

"We're getting married", Emily gasped.

"Wow! Did he propose? Down on one knee? I want all the details."

"Not exactly. It just seemed to happen. I'm not even sure how. But it's real, I'm getting married. You're the first to know. Now I have to tell my parents, and I'm really worried that they won't approve."

"What makes you say that? I thought your parents liked him. You didn't say anything to give me any other impression."

"Well, they seem to have reservations. Believe it or not, they think he is too charming. It got my mother's hackles up. I'm not sure why."

"Seems strange. He's always such good company, the life and soul of any party. In a way, he acts as a foil for you as you're so much more restrained. He brings out the fun side of you. I can't see why that should be a criticism," said Suzanne.

"I'm going to phone them now and tell them my news. I hope they don't go mad. On one hand, they're always pushing me to get married and settle down, but then they don't approve of my choice. It's certainly very complicated. Wish me luck."

Emily sat herself down in her favourite chair and dialled her parents' number. Her mother answered straight away, and when she heard her daughter's voice, she immediately launched into a series of questions about how the holiday had gone. It was difficult for Emily to get a word in edgeways, but finally, she managed to interrupt the never-ending flow of chatter.

"We're getting married, Mum. I'm so excited. I never expected this to happen. It was such a surprise, but I'm so happy I just want to shout and scream and jump up and down," she finally managed to say.

There was a silence at the other end of the phone, and Emily honestly thought the line had gone dead. Finally, her mother breathed out with a long sigh.

"I'm not sure about this. I want to be happy for you, but I'm really not certain whether he is the man for you. You know I'm not totally convinced about him. There's just something which is holding me back. Let me talk to your father about this, and I'll phone you back in a few minutes. Please be patient. I'm really sorry that I have these doubts. It seems to be raining on your parade, but marriage has been going on for a long, long time. You need to be absolutely certain."

Emily felt that someone had pricked her with a pin, and she had totally deflated, just like a burst balloon. She felt the tears welling up and was unable to speak, so she just put the phone down and went to her bedroom. She had been so excited and happy, and now all that feeling had dissipated, leaving her wretched and confused. The misery she felt quickly turned to anger. Why did her mother think she knew better? Surely she, Emily, was a better judge of the man? She was the one who had spent time with him, talked to him, and saw his foibles, his weaknesses and strengths. He was not perfect, certainly, but then neither was she. Her mother's attitude was definitely not valid, and she was determined that she and Seth would marry despite her parents. She didn't need their agreement, permission or even validation, though that would be truly wonderful.

Seth must not know what was going on, that her parents considered him far from ideal as a partner for their daughter. This was a problem for her to sort out, and she alone.

Emily made herself a hot drink and sat in the chair, feeling very deflated from her previous high and waited for the phone to ring. It did finally, and she quickly picked it up, not knowing what was going to happen in the next few minutes.

"Your father and I have discussed it, and we've decided that we are going to give you our full support. I won't deny that we're not 100% delighted at the prospect, but we're going to trust your judgment. After all, you know him so much better than us. You must understand that our doubts were based on our desire for you to be happy, and the niggling reservations were just based on a gut feeling, nothing more."

"I'm so happy, Mum. Having your support is vital to me and always has been. We now need to make plans to tell everyone our news, including Seth's family, though I don't think they really care one way or another."

Emily put the phone down, letting out a long sigh of relief. She had not realised how tense she had been waiting for her parents' reply, but now she felt the stiffness from her shoulders disappear and her whole body relaxed. She laughed out loud in a loud burst of delight, dancing around the room out of sheer happiness. She couldn't wait to speak to Seth, although she obviously could not let him know about her parents' reservations. That would have to remain her secret. She needed her future husband and her family to be one with each other, and she knew that time would dissipate her parents' lack of enthusiasm for the match. They would see Seth for the kind, caring man that he was and for his outgoing personality, which was positive and had no hidden agendas as they had feared.

Emily sat daydreaming about the future, what needed to be done, weddings and bridal dresses. There was such confusion of thoughts that she decided that she would really have to resort to making lists, which was not something she usually did. There was so much to organise, but first of all, she needed to make up her mind as to the type of wedding she really wanted.

Since the debacle of her twenty-first birthday party, Emily has not changed her attitude toward big parties. She hated them! Her shyness and continuing lack of self-confidence held her back in a big crowd. She had no idea how to make small talk to people she hardly knew or 'work a room', so she quickly appreciated that this wedding would have to be a small affair comprising just close family and friends. She didn't know how this would go down with her parents, who had long dreamed of a big fancy 'do' to rival those of their friends. She would have to fight her corner. She knew most girls grew up making plans for the big day, planning the dress, choosing the venue and the music, but she had never done this. There were no preconceptions. She would have to start from scratch.

Sitting by the open window with the sun streaming its warmth onto her, Emily's mind began to drift into a fantasy of hope and desire. Images of white gowns, smiling faces and laughter became a background of paradise and a future filled with love and happiness. She entered into a dream world of perfection. Pictures of laughing children, an adoring husband and a beautiful home swirled around in her head. Could such perfection be achieved? Could it really happen, or was she just hoping for an unattainable illusion? Surely everybody who entered into marriage with their chosen loved one experienced the same hopes and visions? Seth was such good fun, made her laugh and was a perfect foil for her more reserved personality. His support would lead her to the confidence she so longed for. The future looked good. What could go wrong?

Emily also knew that her well-to-do parents had planned for her future, and a deposit for a house would be forthcoming. Nothing could be expected from Seth's family, but that was not a problem. She, too, had always been a saver and had a considerable sum saved and invested, which could now be used to help fund a home and a future together. Seth had no money. She knew that, but she was happy to underwrite their life together. After all, marriage should be an equal partnership with both partners willing to share and combine. It would be an excellent investment. In time, hopefully, Seth would also get his career on track, rise through the ranks of whichever profession he finally settled in, and be able to contribute to the finances of the marriage on an equal basis. For now, she would just have to bear the brunt of the load. Shaking herself out of her daydream, she took out a notebook and pen and started to make lists.

While she was deep into making decisions about what needed to be done and thought about, her parents were deep in a conversation about the forthcoming nuptials, which they found profoundly troubling.

"Am I just being awkward, or is there really something to worry about here?" asked her mother. 'I just don't trust him. There is something not quite right about this young man. It's just a feeling I have. I'm terrified that she is jumping into a situation which could be problematic. I know that we haven't always been close as mother and daughter, but I thought we had now ironed out all our problems and that I could be honest with her. What's your take on the situation?"

Her husband thought carefully and talked slowly, thinking his way through the minefield of his wife's words. Like many men, he wasn't too keen on facing an emotional situation head-on but knew that on this occasion, he couldn't avoid it.

"At first, I didn't have the same doubts as you did, but that time when they missed the train was very worrying for me. It made me reconsider my opinion of him, but I can't really come down hard on Emily to take a step backwards. I think we're just going to have to take a deep breath, accept this marriage, and pray that it works out well. She is totally convinced by him and is totally blind to his failings. If we say anything, I think she will be so offended that she may remove herself from our orbit, and we will have lost our daughter."

"That's my worry also, which is why I gave her my blessing, provisional though it was, and we just have to hope that she is right and we are wrong. I just want what any parent wants for their child – for her to be happy and fulfilled, but I can envisage many sleepless nights worrying about it."

CHAPTER 11

Just as Emily had predicted, Seth's parents reacted as anticipated to the news that their son was entering into matrimony with a total lack of interest. They said the right things but seemed disassociated from the whole matter. Emily was somewhat disappointed despite having known that this would be their attitude but had hoped that marriage in the family would help build bridges. She decided to put the issue aside and look forward positively, deeply immersed in planning the coming wedding and finding somewhere to live, both matters of greater importance than dealing with disinterested future in-laws. After all, she was marrying Seth and not his parents.

She spent many hours with her mother, a very capable person who threw herself into wedding plans with seemingly great enthusiasm. Emily decided to let her get on with it, leaving time and space for her and Seth to house hunt. Before these plans had matured, Seth landed a bombshell on her. He had been offered a superior position in the university library in Manchester. This would be a big step upward, and he was keen to take the job. There was nothing really standing in their way. Emily, after all, could find a job as a teacher in Manchester, which was why she had gone to university to attain her qualifications. This was the advantage of having such a career. It gave flexibility and the opportunity to work almost anywhere. They spent a long time discussing it and decided to go for it. The timing was good as the wedding plans were well advanced, and they could move north immediately after the wedding, find somewhere to buy, and start married life in a new community. In addition, property prices were considerably lower there, which would give them more scope, and their money would go much further.

It was very exciting, but it was a huge change for both of them. Emily had discussed with her flatmate what would happen when she left their shared home. Suzanne told her that she had sounded out a couple of friends who were looking to find a new place to live, so Emily didn't need to worry about that score. All would be well. There were other issues, of course. Their family and friends lived in 'swinging' London. The city was well-known to them and was a place bursting with excitement, adventure, culture and opportunity. How would provincial Manchester compare? Surely they would miss being so close to their family, particularly Emily? The idea was certainly very daunting, and she felt very apprehensive about such a huge change in her circumstances. Seth would travel north to find temporary accommodation while Emily stayed in London to sort out all the details for the wedding, especially finding a stunning gown for the big day.

As she had expected, her parents wanted a huge, fancy affair. Emily made it very plain that this was just what she did not want. They came to a compromise on a smaller function of delicious lunch and smart tea later in the afternoon. All were happy with this, and now all that was needed was to get it sorted. After all, it would save her parents a small fortune! Emily found a fabulous dress which would be made for her. She went for fittings and amazed the dressmaker with her unbelievably small build. The gown would be an elegant sheath, not at all the big blancmange that was so fashionable at that time.

She also sorted out wedding rings for the two of them. Seth would pay for these, he promised, and they were being made for them by a jeweller her father knew well. Hers, in particular, was very up to the minute in design, and she couldn't wait to wear it, put on her finger by the man she intended to spend the rest of her life with. Emily's excitement mounted, and she walked around in a daydream and a haze of euphoria that she had never experienced in her entire life before.

Seth left for Manchester, and she missed him so badly. They phoned each night, talking the evening away, joking and laughing and making their plans. Seth declared his deep passion for her over and over, but Emily could not hear enough of it. She was so lucky to have found such a man, and she knew he would always be at her side, protecting and supporting her. He would come down that weekend to spend a couple of days together. While they were separated, Seth would search for temporary accommodation for them. After the wedding, they would have the space and time to find a home to buy together in which they could start their joint life. The rings would also be ready for collection, and they could do this together.

Friday came, and Emily went to the station to meet Seth. She threw herself into his welcoming arms, and they clutched each other as though they had not met for months. When she finally disentangled her mouth from his, she told him that they would go straight to the jeweller to collect the rings.

"I can't wait to see them", he said. Emily tried to describe hers to him but laughed at his confused look.

"You'll soon see it. It's going to be so gorgeous and unusual, not just a plain, boring band like yours," she teased.

"I'm not into fancy jewellery. It's enough that I agreed to wear a wedding ring. Not many men do, you know."

They arrived at the workshop, and the jeweller brought out the rings and placed them both on velvet pads to show them off to full effect. Seth's was just a plain gold band, as he had requested, but hers shimmered with the bark effect in white and yellow gold, which was so fashionable at this time. Emily picked it up, overwhelmed by how well it had turned out, much more beautiful than she had ever dreamed.

They were told the price to pay, and Emily turned to Seth as he was footing the bill. He felt around for his wallet and then searched more thoroughly.

"I think I must have left it behind in Manchester," he said. "I'm so sorry, my darling. Could you lay it out? I will let you have the money back, I promise."

Emily was somewhat taken aback but reached into her bag and took out her chequebook. She wrote the amount and tore it out, handing it to the jeweller.

"Don't worry. Just pay me back when you find your wallet. It's not a problem. Luckily, there is plenty of money in my account to cover the cost of the rings."

They left the shop together, hand in hand, to return to Emily's flat to spend the evening quietly, catching up for the time they had spent apart. Seth was still apologising for his lack of funds to pay for the rings and promising over and over that he would let her have the money very soon.

The weekend passed all too quickly. On Sunday morning, Seth left the flat early to buy the weekend paper plus bagels and smoked salmon, as was their usual weekend routine. They spent the day companionably reading the paper, followed by a long walk in the local park, and the afternoon was concluded with tea and cream cakes in the park café overlooking the lake. They watched the ducks, which they so enjoyed doing, laughing at their antics and throwing them pieces of cake, which they gobbled up, fighting and squabbling with each other in their bid to capture the titbits.

The afternoon was finally over, and Seth had to return to the station to catch the train back up north. Emily wandered home slowly, clutching the rings and feeling disconsolate at the separation but knowing that they would soon be together permanently, never to be parted. Seth had found a reasonable flat for them both in Manchester, which was in tolerable condition, and he was giving it a bit of an update to make it more habitable and to their taste. He had consulted Emily about colours, and he was determined to get it right, he assured her.

The big day arrived. All had gathered at Emily's parents' house, except Seth, of course. The bride appeared, and all caught their breath. They started to clap and laugh at the elegant, sophisticated vision in front of them. The simple sheath of white silk clung to Emily's body like a second skin. Her hair was caught up in a simple diadem of white flowers, which held her short veil in place. Her bouquet of mixed white flowers accented with pale lemon roses reflected the total image of style and beauty. Her father walked forward, took her hand in his, and gently kissed it, too emotional to say even a single word. The smile on his face and the tears in his eyes were a projection of the deep pride and love he held for his beloved child.

He led her to the hired car, bedecked with white ribbons that fluttered in the warm breeze, helping her to settle herself with her dress carefully arranged so as not to crush it, and then he sat by her side as the chauffeur closed the door of the car and they set off to the country club not too far away where the ceremony would take place in the beautiful gardens under a rose-covered pergola.

Seth was waiting for her, and his parents were nearby, who appeared to have made an effort to look the part of the groom's family. Emily was relieved to see that they were nicely dressed and smiled at them, kissing them on the cheek. All would be well, she thought as Seth took his place at the front and the music started. Her father held her arm and handed her to the husband-to-be, and the ceremony began. The celebrant, a middle-aged man dressed in a smart grey suit, smiled at the two of them as they stood before him. The words flowed, and the bride and groom made their wedding vows, which they had written together amid much laughter the week before. They committed themselves to a life of togetherness and mutual love and devotion and the start of many years of happiness and fulfilment. Just as fast as it had begun, suddenly it was over, and she heard the words 'you may kiss the bride'. Seth held her briefly, gave her a light kiss and moved away. He looked around him and started chatting to one of his friends. She stood alone.

Emily was confused. What was happening? They had just been joined in holy matrimony, and her new husband was behaving as though they had just come out of the cinema.

She gazed at him but said nothing. She walked up to him and took his arm as they were overwhelmed by good wishes and hugs and kisses of congratulations. Maybe she had imagined it all. Nobody else seemed to have noticed. He came to her side to sign the wedding register, making them legally married in the eyes of the law. Emily felt very strange signing her new name. This would take some getting used to, she mused.

The wedding party proceeded smoothly. The bride and groom, their parents and friends moved to the large marquee where the tables had been set for the lunch. Flowers abounded, and a trio played music in the background, not too loudly as yet. That would come later when the bride and groom took to the dance floor. The food was delicious, the music fun and the party went with a swing. Emily felt throughout that she was alone in all this, isolated and confused. This was definitely not what she had anticipated or imagined. Seth hardly bothered with her, barely looking at her or saying very much at all. What was going on? She had no idea. This should have been the happiest day of her life, but instead, she was steeped in misery and confusion. She chatted with people and smiled when they told her how beautiful she looked and wished her well in her new life. Her parents were wonderful hosts and seemed unaware of their daughter's misery. Emily continued to play her part as the supremely happy, blushing bride, hiding the turmoil within her. She could say nothing. Nobody must know, especially not her parents. She had been married just a couple of hours, and she was already wondering if she had made the mistake of a lifetime. And Seth had not given her the money for the rings either, she thought bitterly.

People started to say their goodbyes, and the music wound down. The chatter also faded, and Seth suddenly came over and took her in his arms, kissing her so deeply. With such love and passion, she started to think that she had misread the situation and imagined all the preceding events. It must all have been a huge mirage. She said nothing but melted into his arms, once again happy and contented to be his wife. Maybe he had been overwhelmed by the whole occasion and unable to cope with the attention, though usually, it was she who did not like to be at the epicentre of a social setting. She mentally shook herself, gazed at her new husband and smiled contentedly. Laughing, they ran hand-in-hand to the car to drive to the hotel, showered with confetti and rose petals, where they were to spend their wedding night.

CHAPTER 12

The newlyweds had decided against an immediate honeymoon, or rather Seth had. He considered that the move to Manchester was such a massive one and also expensive that they should just settle in there and leave the holiday for a later date. He promised Emily that they would certainly have a trip abroad in the very near future, just not at the present time. Seth had settled into his new job, which did not appear to be very demanding, and Emily soon found herself a post at a local secondary school within easy walking distance of their home, so the future looked promising. They knew no one and had no friends in the city, which was something of a shock after their madcap social life in London. Nevertheless, they hoped friends would come up from London on the occasional weekend to nose around their new home, and they would travel down to London to stay with Emily's parents and catch up with all the news and gossip.

As expected, Emily's parents had been more than generous in handing over a substantial sum with which to set up a home. Arriving at their new temporary flat, they found that her mother had had a huge delivery of everything required to fill the kitchen cupboards and the fridge. They would not go hungry, that was for sure. Also, as expected, Seth's parents contributed nothing at all despite promises to the contrary. Seth never mentioned this lack of input to the new home, and Emily did not consider it of sufficient importance to bring the matter up, so nothing was said. After all, they were so lucky that so much had been given to them to make a substantial start. Not many newlyweds were so fortunate.

Seth had settled in his new job, and Emily soon found herself a post at a local secondary school within easy walking distance of their home, so the future looked promising. Despite knowing no one in the city, their friends, as anticipated, came up from London from time to time, and they would also travel down to London.

On the first Sunday in their new home, Emily went into the kitchen to put the kettle on, expecting Seth to go out and buy rolls, salmon and the Sunday papers. He did not do so. He lay in bed luxuriating in the peace and quiet that a lie-in could give him. It was nearly lunchtime before he hauled himself out of bed and dressed when Emily called him to the table to eat something. It was their first full weekend in their shared home, and she thought that he wanted to relish the feeling of a new freedom, so made no comment.

“What would you like to do today?” he asked her as he finished the last bit of food on the plate.

“Perhaps we could explore the surrounding area and see what’s doing. Maybe there are some parks or trendy pubs we could visit and check out the shops. But we need to do the dishes first,” she replied.

“All right, I’ll go and have a shower while you clear up,” he said. He vanished in the direction of the bathroom, totally impervious to the atmosphere he had created.

Emily stared after him, open-mouthed, as he went into the bathroom. She looked at the pile of dishes and realised no help was coming from her new husband and set to with the dishmop and washing-up liquid. This was certainly not turning out the way she had envisaged, she thought as she slopped water and banged dishes all over the place in a fury of shock and frustration.

After a decent interval, all the mess of the meal having been cleared away, Seth duly appeared, grabbed her round the waist and danced her around the kitchen.

“Let’s go out. It’s such a lovely afternoon; the sun is shining, and I’m married to the most wonderful woman in the world.”

His laughter banished her blues clean away, and she nodded enthusiastically. They put on light jackets, stared at the sky and decided to take rain gear as certain clouds looked as though they might be threatening rain at some point. They ran down the stairs hand in hand, wandering the streets until they found a pretty park with a pond and the inevitable wildfowl. There was even a circular bandstand with a large brass band playing popular music. The musicians were in the full uniform gear of navy jackets with gold buttons and epaulettes, peaked hats with gold badges, and red trim. Their navy trousers had a broad white stripe down the outside of the legs, and they certainly looked the business.

Emily and Seth bought ice cream cones with a flake stuck in them, found deckchairs and settled down to enjoy the entertainment. They sang along where they could and tapped their feet, clapping enthusiastically at the end of each number. Even the rain stayed away. After a while, they sauntered off to explore the gardens, which were well-kept and in full, glorious bloom. The afternoon was finished off sitting in companionable silence with tea and scones in the little café, feeding crumbs to the sparrows who descended in large droves to peck at the offerings at their feet.

This was definitely the life, mused Emily, totally putting behind her his disheartening behaviour of earlier in the day. She would have to get used to her husband's peculiar conduct at times and learn to live with it. His ability to ignore his deeds and move on with no apology or mention was strange in the extreme. She had never encountered such an attitude and could not understand where it was coming from.

The day ended on a high, and the weeks that followed were filled with work and play, love and laughter and a feeling of togetherness and unity, which gave Emily great joy. She felt as though all was well with her world despite the niggling hiccups she had experienced on the way. Maybe she had overthought them or even imagined them, but it was certainly true that the consideration that had preceded the marriage in many ways had disappeared. For instance, Seth's pre-marriage habit of bringing in delicious items for breakfast at the weekend, together with a choice of newspapers, had disappeared into the ether. Emily missed this but kept her mouth shut. She did not want to appear critical or a nag. His promises also seemed to him of no import. Basically, he never kept them. He had never paid for the wedding rings, and he would often offer to pick up something at the shops but would return without the item, saying he had forgotten it, with a shrug of his shoulders and no apology or comment.

She discussed these misgivings with no one. Her parents had not been altogether happy with her choice of life partner, and she desperately did not want them to know that maybe they were right and she was wrong. Nor did she talk to Suzanne or any other friends about what was going on in her life. After all, nobody was perfect. She certainly was not, and realistically, she could not expect that from Seth. Surely, these were minor considerations and criticisms. Generally speaking, she was content and in love, and she felt loved in return. Her job was developing nicely, and she was gaining experience in her new career. She seemed popular with both children and staff. Her dreams were still intact.

Emily started to make friends among the teachers she worked with in the school. She particularly seemed to make a connection with another new member of staff, similar in age to herself, called Harriet, who had started at the school on the same day as she did. As a result, they were thrown together quite a bit and sat together at lunchtime when they ate their sandwiches in the staff room. Both being new to the job, they experienced many of the same niggles and problems of dealing with a roomful of stroppy teenagers who seemed to delight in getting a rise from the poor, benighted young woman standing at the front of the class trying to impart their knowledge to a new generation.

"What does one do when someone starts to undermine you with snide remarks whispered loudly to the girl in front of her?" asked Harriet.

"I came into the classroom and found an exact replica of my signature on the blackboard," Emily said, "so I just laughed and complimented the forger, and the culprit put her hand up."

"Definitely, you can't let them get to you. The slightest sign of weakness and they will be on to you like a pack of hounds. I think I'm starting to win their respect, though. If you can get them interested in the subject without being heavy-handed, then I think we should make it through," she laughed.

The two young women lived close to each other, just a couple of streets apart, so they fell into the habit of meeting on the corner in the morning and walking home together at the end of the school day. Harriet was also newly married to David, and they planned to meet up as a foursome quite soon. Emily told Seth about her new friend, and he seemed keen to get to know the new couple. They made an arrangement to meet at Emily's home over the weekend.

Harriet was tall and slim, fair-haired and very attractive. She was outgoing and lively, liked to sing and was joining a local choir and tried to encourage Emily to come along too.

"You'll meet lots of new people. You're new to this city, and it can be lonely. It would also be really fun to have you there. We don't sing the heavy stuff, just music from the shows, folk music, pop music and stuff like that. We do perform at concerts, but it's pretty low-key, and most of the audience is made up of friends and family who tend to be very forgiving!"

"Don't you have to read music?" Emily asked. "I did learn to play the piano, but I don't think I can sight read music. And don't you have to have an audition? I think that would terrify me."

"No. Neither one. It's called a Community Choir, so it's open to all. We just have a lot of fun, and it's a terrific way of meeting people of all types from different places and jobs. It's very egalitarian. Please try it out. And what about Seth? He might be interested also."

“It sounds like a great idea. Let’s discuss it when you come over at the weekend and take it from there.”

They had agreed to meet on Saturday evening. Emily would prepare a light supper, and Harriet and her husband would bring the wine and dessert so that Emily would not have to make too much of an effort. Seth seemed to have opted out of helping with cooking, although occasionally, he would help with the washing up. He had been brought up to consider that this was ‘women’s work’ though Emily planned to gradually change his perception of the role each had to play within a marriage. She remembered the battle her friend Daisy had had with her husband to let her achieve her desire to further herself. They were no longer living in the Victorian era. Women had come of age, and times had dramatically changed. Many men, unfortunately, had not noticed the difference that feminism had brought to the world and believed that there had been no change in the status quo.

Right on time, the doorbell rang, and Emily opened the door to let in her friend. This was the first time she had met Harriet’s husband. He was definitely a terrific foil to his elegant wife. He was good-looking and had a smile that was warm and friendly. Seth came to shake hands with the couple, and Emily noticed her husband taking a long, calculating look at her friend, who, as always, looked gorgeous. He quickly checked himself and gave Harriet a kiss on the cheek to welcome her. They all went into the living room for drinks and nibbles and to get to know each other.

The talk went easily as they found much in common, and soon they went to sit around the table to carry on chatting and raising a glass to new friendships and new beginnings. All too soon, the evening came to an end, and goodbyes were said after they had made arrangements to go to the cinema to see the latest blockbuster, M*A*S*H, which they were all dying to see. The evening had been a great success, and Emily and Seth even cheerfully helped to clear the table and wash up while she dried and put the dishes in the correct cupboards. Emily was looking forward to seeing the relationship between the two couples flourish. This was the first time she and Seth were making a connection with another twosome from scratch, and she found it all rather exciting. It also made her feel very married.

“I liked them”, Seth commented. “I think we can really make good friends out of them. We seem to have a lot in common and a good foundation to build on.”

"It's the first time I've met David. They seem such a devoted couple. He has a really kind face and a lovely warm nature. He is totally obsessed with his wife. It's so nice to see such a terrific relationship. They remind me of my parents. I'm so glad you also liked them."

Even while she was speaking, Emily understood the irony of what she had just said. It was definitely not true of her relationship with Seth, and she felt a niggle of real disappointment and envy in the stark difference between the two pairs.

"I'm looking forward to getting to know them better and hopefully having fun together. It will also help to expand our communal circle. After all our friends in London, we need to build up a better social life here in Manchester," Seth continued.

The four of them started to meet regularly at each others' homes but also went out together at the weekend. They all liked hiking, and the countryside around Manchester was truly glorious, with so many opportunities to explore. Trips to the sea were also on the agenda, picnics by the water's edge sitting on a freezing cold beach wrapped in blankets and drinking wine and beer to try and keep warm. It was very British, but life was fun.

Harriet and her husband David also introduced them to their circle of friends, and soon, their social life began to expand, which proved to be very satisfactory. Emily's teaching career was developing nicely, and she found it a great deal of work with all the lesson preparation necessary together with the volume of marking, but she found her pupils delightful and rewarding. And they seemed to like her! Life was truly wonderful, with a loving husband and a great job. There were moments, certainly, which Emily found strange and unsettling. Seth would sometimes come out with a very caustic comment or put her down in front of their friends. Why did he do that? Their friends did not seem to notice, or were too polite to comment. But they seemed to like him, and he certainly turned on the charm, especially to Harriet, but Emily felt safe in his love of her and just laughed when Seth complimented Harriet particularly or put his arm around her possessively. Nothing untoward was going on. Emily knew that. It was just his way.

The end of the year was fast approaching, and the group of friends, now numbering eight, were discussing how they should celebrate the occasion. They knew the city was putting on a huge fireworks display. Should they go to that or mark the occasion differently?

"I think it's high time we had a party. We could have it here, couldn't we, Emily?" Seth said.

"Why not, though we don't have space for a horde of people, maybe twenty at most. If everybody brought some food and drink, it would be affordable and easier for me. We could use paper plates and disposable cutlery and glasses. I don't really want to spend the day preparing and serving and cleaning up all night. What do you all think?" she replied.

"Good idea, and we will need decorations too. And what about the music? Who would be in charge of that? I have a lot of great tapes, but we could pool what we have, which would give us a greater variety," another joined in.

The group started to make lists of what needed to be done and who would do what. They were all starting out in life and did not have much money to spend, but by spreading the load, nobody would have to fork out too much. Having made all the decisions, they got down to the serious business of drinking, smoking and having fun until they straggled homeward to fall into bed with the plans buzzing in their minds. It would be a great New Year and something to look forward to. 1971, here we come, was Emily's last thought as her head hit the pillow.

The days seemed to race by. School broke up for the Christmas holidays, and Emily and Seth spent the holidays in London with her parents. Emily caught up with her friends and those that Seth had. It had been a fun break, but now it was time to return home and prepare for the party.

CHAPTER 13

All was set. Music blared out, filling the room and probably the whole building with the sound of Led Zepellin. Emily hoped the neighbours would not complain, although she had had the forethought to let them know of the plans for the party. They were mainly a young crowd and told her that she shouldn't worry, they had their own plans for the evening. The table was set, and friends were starting to gather, piling their offerings onto the table, and bottles of drink and beer joined the rest on the drinks table or were stashed in the fridge to keep nice and cold.

Harriet and David arrived, she looking gorgeous as ever and David more laid back but stylish. Emily herself wore a black, tight, very short mini dress cut very low at the back with long, shiny black boots. She had piled on masses of gold necklaces, bracelets and rings bought cheaply at the local market, which made her look exotic, trendy and definitely up-to-the-minute fashion-wise. She wore her hair piled up on top with tendrils falling loosely around her face and decorated with yet more gold stars until she became a glittering vision of glamorous allure. Seth held her in his arms, kissed her bare back and told her how stunning she was and how proud he was to be her husband. Emily glowed in his approval.

David looked round the room, now buzzing with guests. "This is going to be a huge success. And you look amazing, Emily. I love all the jewellery. You certainly have a good eye on how to put things together in a different way. Fabulous," he said.

"Well, New Year's eve is a special occasion. I'm not usually into parties, but I'm certainly going to make the most of this one and have a smashing time. Seth also seems to appreciate the effort Harriet has put in judging by the way he is gazing at her," Emily laughed.

The two friends looked over at their spouses, Seth bending in to talk in Harriet's ear, close because of the thumping music, now The Who.

"I think we'll have to keep an eye on them," David said, looking thoughtful.

"That's ridiculous. She adores you, and I trust Seth implicitly. We are newly married, you know," she replied.

People were helping themselves to the food and the drinks table was emptying at an alarming rate, with a consequent rise in decibels due to the throng starting to become somewhat inebriated. Emily hoped the drinks would last, but she certainly had no intention of going out to buy more. What was there would have to do. Anyway, she did not want anybody throwing up or becoming objectionable due to having poured too much alcohol inside themselves. Seth, she knew, liked his whisky and she decided she would keep watch to see that he did not drink too much of it. He had a tendency to become loud and happy when drunk but not aggressive. He also became more loving, although the more he professed his undying love for her due to inebriation, his capacity to perform diminished proportionately, she had found!

The television was on showing fireworks displays around the world until finally it became time for the UK, and the cameras panned to shots of Big Ben and the crowds on the Embankment and in Trafalgar Square and the countdown began.

Ten, nine, eight, seven, six, five, four, three, two, one. Happy New Year! Seth grabbed her in his arms, kissing and hugging her and Auld Lang Syne was sung loudly and drunkenly. Emily turned to receive chaste kisses from their friends, and out of the corner of her eye, she glimpsed Seth holding Harriet in a hold which could only be described as 'passionate'. She stood still and watched, her gaze fixed on what she saw unfolding before her. Then Harriet seemed to pull away, and Seth whispered something in her ear, but Harriet turned her back on him and went to find her husband. Emily was stunned but had no time to consider what had happened as she was spun round by yet another friend wanting to wish her a happy new year. She shrugged her shoulders and decided she was imagining what she had seen and was overreacting. After all, she and Seth were married and he was constantly telling her of his commitment and love for her. She would say nothing.

The revelry continued well into the early hours, though the music was now Joni Mitchell and the tone of the evening had changed to a quieter, more thoughtful mood. People were sprawled on the furniture and the floor, chatting quietly and uttering philosophical thoughts spawned by alcohol, which made them consider themselves experts in so many fields. The ills of the world were being analyzed, and solutions to age-old problems were brought forward. Of course, the imminent introduction of decimal currency in about six weeks' time was the hot topic, with many laughing at the attitude of some who considered this should not come into force 'until all the old people had died'. Would it lead to inflation? Would they be cheated and conned, especially vulnerable people? Of course, no conclusions were reached although strong opinions aired.

Finally, everybody drifted their way home, and Seth and Emily were left to assess the clearing up and the potential damage to their home. Seth told her it could all wait till the morning, but she sorted out the worst of it, piling everything in heaps in the kitchen and went to join her husband in the bedroom.

Lying in bed, her thoughts went back to what she had seen. Harriet had obviously been unwilling to co-operate with whatever Seth had suggested. That was demonstrated by her body language. But what had he been whispering in her ear? And why did he clutch Harriet so passionately? Was it the drink talking, and was that just an excuse or justifiable? Emily's mind was whirling, unable to decide what to do or say. This was so new to her, and she had no idea how to approach the matter, even if at all.

She lay on her back and found herself crying quietly. Seth was talking to her, wanting to celebrate the New Year in a timely fashion but she ignored his approaches.

"What's the matter?" he asked.

"I'm not happy with how the party went and the attention you were paying to Harriet" she blurted out.

"I don't want to hear that," he answered, and his fist shot out and punched her in the face, hard. Totally stunned, but before she could do or say anything, he grabbed her by her shoulders and forced himself onto her. She shouted at him to stop, leave her alone. He ignored her cries and was totally silent. She struggled and fought, but he grabbed both her wrists and held them down above her head so she was helpless while he thrust into her violently and ruthlessly until he climaxed, rolled off her, turned his back on her and fell asleep. She lay there, violated and hurting, both physically and emotionally, totally unable to move or even breathe properly.

Emily was dumbfounded. She could not think. What had just happened? Never in her life had she experienced violence. The concept was totally alien to her. Her parents' marriage was one of love and mutual respect. She knew from the papers that these things happened, but how was it happening to her? What should she do? Could she do anything? How could she get help or discuss it with anyone? She dared not tell her parents after their doubts about Seth. They had seen something in him she had not recognised and she could not now tell them they had been right all along. The shame would be too great and she was now stuck in a situation with no way out. He would apologize in the morning. She was sure of that. How could they move forward from this, and could she forgive him?

One thing she was certain about. Their relationship was permanently damaged and she would never, ever, tell him her most intimate thoughts again. What sort of marriage would it be if openness was off the table? She was trapped. Despite the advances in society and the forward movement of women's rights, domestic violence was hardly mentioned. Men could get into a fight in the pub and the assailant dragged to the police station and given a prison sentence for violence. But a woman could be beaten senseless on a regular basis and the police and other authorities would turn a blind eye, shrugging their collective shoulders, saying it was a 'personal matter' and a 'domestic' between husband and wife and it was not their place to interfere.

Her thoughts were in turmoil. She had read that there were women who were trying to change this state of affairs, but it was in its infancy and certainly would be of no good to her. The humiliation of coming forward would be too extreme. Marriage in 1971 was an unequal partnership with differing rights in a society where the man was the head of the household, and women were the underdog. Emily was trapped, and she knew it. Her dreams and hopes for the future had now disappeared into thin air.

She lay in the bed, her mind abuzz with the horror of what had transpired. She turned and twisted but finally fell into a disturbed, patchy sleep with nightmares that frightened and shook her. Morning finally came.

Emily crawled out of bed, careful not to disturb Seth who was breathing quietly, still fast asleep. She went into the bathroom and, locked the door behind her and looked in the mirror. She gazed in horror at her face. Her right eye was swollen and half shut. Blue and purple filled the eye socket. She touched it gently with her forefinger and winced at the pain. She had a black eye. What on earth was she going to do?

She considered herself to be a cut above in society, not being inclined to go down the pub, get into fights and roll home drunk. Now, she was no different from the segment of society she had always despised and looked down on. She was one of them. An abused woman. A statistic. What on earth was she going to do? How to move forward from this horror?

Emily brought out her make-up bag and rummaged around in it until she found the heavy-duty concealer she scarcely had ever used. She certainly needed it now. She slathered the concealer around her eye and smoothed it down, gently applied foundation and then finished the job with mascara and eye shadow. Would anyone be able to notice? It appeared acceptable, but it was not the time of year to hide behind dark glasses. Thank goodness it was the school holidays, and it would be a few days before she had to face a class. She prayed that the bruising would fade before that day arrived.

She sat on the toilet seat, considering her options. They seemed to be few and left not much room for choice. She realised she was stuck in a situation that she loathed, but there seemed little in practice that she could do except plough on with what was becoming something of a farce of a relationship. She also started to think back to her time with Seth and the issues which had niggled at her, which she had refused to deal with head-on. There was the time they had missed the train; he had also never paid for the wedding rings and all the other failed promises. Things were starting to add up and she now saw where her parents were coming from in their distrust of her choice of husband.

But how should she deal with it in practical terms? That was the conundrum. The worst was that she loved him.

CHAPTER 14

She continued to sit on the loo, staring blankly at the far wall and considering her options. She really could not work out how to move on and deal with the situation. She heard the sounds of Seth getting up, and she quickly unlocked the bathroom door and walked out into the bedroom. Her husband beamed at her!

"What a great party that was. Maybe we should make it an annual event. Everybody seemed to really be enjoying themselves. I hope you did, too. You were certainly the most beautiful woman in the room, and I was so proud of you," he said.

Emily stared at him in horror. Was she hallucinating? Was he truly ignoring what had happened, that he had punched her in the face? And raped her. How could this be? She did not answer him but walked over to the wardrobe to take clean clothes out for the day. He came up behind her and put his arms around her, leaning his face into her neck. She felt herself stiffen, unable to bear his touch, which seemed to be burning her flesh away where it made contact.

"Come back to bed, and let's celebrate the New Year in proper fashion," he continued. He led her to the bed, where she lay down, wondering what was going on. Surely this was not happening? How could he ignore what had done to her? He started to touch her in the way he knew she liked. In bed, making love, he was gentle, considerate, thoughtful and very good. Now was no exception. Much to her annoyance, despite her misery and fury, she felt her body responding. She had a high libido, and being hit in the face did not seem to have affected it.

When they had both climaxed, they lay together in the bed, Seth holding her gently. He was talking to her quietly, discussing what they should do that day.

"Where shall we go today? We should start the new year in style, I think. Maybe out to lunch and then a walk in the woods. Don't you agree?" She was silent. Once again he was totally ignoring the elephant in the room. The pattern now could be clearly seen. He would behave badly but seemed to have no recollection of what he had done. Was this real or was it an act? Ignore the issue, and it will disappear. She was bewildered, not understanding his behaviour. There was absolutely no mention of the punch in the face, no apology. In his book, therefore, it had not happened. Or had it?

They cleared up the mess in the kitchen together and tidied the rest of the flat, with Seth chatting cheerfully, seemingly impervious to her mood and lack of response. She sighed deeply and decided she would just have to go with the flow. Either she had to bring the subject up, or the alternative was to put the matter behind her. The choice was bleak. She decided on the latter and hoped it was never repeated.

"I have a great idea. We could go for lunch in that trendy little restaurant down the road which has just opened. The local paper gave it a terrific review. It's worth a try, don't you think?" Seth now said. Coats were found and they wrapped up warmly, armed with somewhat useless umbrellas to stave off the icy winds which were driving the rain almost horizontally. The establishment was a small, family-run eatery where the food and service were good and the prices reasonable. The excellent reviews were definitely justified. They ate their food and then went for a long walk, despite the freezing weather, in a nearby park. They were well protected against the elements with woolly hats, big scarves and fleece-lined boots. Emily found herself relaxing and responding to Seth's chatter despite her rapidly freezing toes. They began to talk about house hunting seriously.

Emily's parents had given her a large sum of money to help them buy a house. Now that they were more settled in Manchester and were getting to know the city, they decided they would start looking for a suitable property, making a large deposit, meaning they would only need a moderate mortgage. The balance of the money would be used to buy furniture and other necessities for a home. They knew they were fortunate compared to many who did not have such a good start in life, not having to scrimp and save. A visit to the bank was planned to sort out a mortgage, and then they could start looking. They wanted a three-bedroom property with a manageable garden in the suburbs of Manchester. They were not sure which area but agreed that they would have a look around the different parts of the city to find somewhere which they both found agreeable to set up home.

They had already made some desultory attempts at house hunting, and so had a good idea of what they could afford. A small three-bedroomed house seemed manageable.

"We definitely must have a garden, and it has to be close to shops and transport. Also, we're not very good at DIY, so it would have to be in reasonable condition, don't you think?" Emily mused.

"I think so. We can always slap a coat of paint on the walls but nothing structural, which would run away with loads of money. It would be great to get out of the flat, though it certainly has served its purpose. But I'm really excited about living in our own house, getting to know the locality, being part of a community and putting down roots. It's a very seductive notion."

They had no plans to start a family as yet, although the issue had never been discussed, family and friends regularly visited from London, so having extra bedrooms would be very helpful. The future would also allow for a nursery, but definitely not for a while yet, Emily hoped.

Seth had never commented on the fact that so much money was coming from Emily's side of the family. He also said nothing about his parents not even giving them a wedding present, though they had promised them money. It had never materialised. He seemed to have no compunction, however, in spending his wife's savings, regularly pleading poverty. He did not earn a high wage, certainly, but together they had sufficient for their needs. Yet he seemed always short of funds having 'forgotten' his wallet at home when it was time to pay in a restaurant or elsewhere. He always promised to pay Emily back but had yet to do so. Emily said nothing and just continued to fork out the sums necessary. Her savings were depleting rapidly, and it was something of a worry to her, but she was hopeful that Seth would climb the career ladder and be able to improve his contribution to their finances.

They decided that the coming week would see a determined effort to find a property. The local newspaper would be bought and the back pages with all the advertisements for houses for sale carefully studied. Then, they would contact agents to view and see what other suitable properties they had on their lists. This was so exciting, and Emily found the punch in the face receding in her memory, although the black eye would take longer to fade while she anticipated this exciting new development in her life. She continued with the concealer, however, hiding the evidence of his attack.

"Let's buy the paper on the way home, and then we can make a start." They found a newsvendor outside the nearby station and bought a copy of the local rag. "We can find a bench and study it. Have you a pen on you, Seth?" Emily said.

They sat side by side on the bench and, scanned the property pages and immediately found a few hopeful options at sensible prices. They knew they could negotiate on prices, but first, they had to find the right house.

“I won’t have much time this week to look. I’m so busy at the library and have a lot on,” Seth said “so could you phone round the agents and check out which are still available and go and see them. Then if you find something appropriate, which you like, then I can come to view it also”.

Emily was somewhat put out by these comments. She had envisioned searching for a home together, not her doing all the groundwork and then Seth swanning in for the fun bit. After having been flat hunting in London, she knew that they would have to look at many properties before finding ‘the one’. The descriptions in the paper often differed drastically from the reality, and a lot of time was wasted viewing useless rubbish. The romance of finding their joint home seemed to be disappearing very rapidly and they had not even begun yet! She said nothing but sighed inwardly. Marriage was certainly not the heavenly conjoining of two people she had dreamed of.

Seth always had a reason for not going to the shops to buy milk/ paper/ bread or anything else at all. In fact, he never even made an excuse, just shrugged his shoulders and ignored her requests. She remembered pre-marriage when he brought her home goodies and little treats. These were now a distant memory. In fact, the only time he showed any consideration was in bed. The moment his foot hit the floor, his nature totally changed. She realised she was not happy, but what could she do? Life was not an idyllic dream, but is anyone's life sheer perfection? As long as the violence did not escalate, she could cope. There was no-one she could talk to, no-one to turn to. She was shamed by the situation she found herself in but too proud to discuss these matters with her parents.

Emily turned her attention back to the paper and circled a few hopefuls. She would phone the estate agents tomorrow as there were still a few days of holiday left until the new term started. It was best to get the train in motion. Maybe having their own home would improve matters by giving a focus and a shared commitment to them both.

CHAPTER 15

Seth returned to work. He said he would be home late that night as there was a lot of re-organising which needed doing at the library, and he had been roped in to help. This gave Emily a free day to start the serious job of house-hunting. She phoned the agents who had advertised in the paper and made appointments to view the properties that interested her. She had circled five, but two had already been put under offer. She sincerely hoped that, being in the fortunate position of a first-time buyer, no long chain would hold them up. There were so many horror stories told of the pitfalls of house purchase and the dreaded 'chain'.

As she had anticipated, most of the properties she saw were non-starters. Either they had a railway running yards from the living room or were literally falling apart. She kept buying the local paper, and agents would phone her with suitable properties. Her brief to them was for a three-bedroom house with a garden, and they would phone her proposing a two-bedroom flat on the third floor with no lift. It was difficult sometimes to hold on to one's temper, but she just calmly reiterated her demands. She knew the perfect home was out there, just waiting for her. She lived in hope.

Seth was arriving home late most evenings apologising for having to work late. He was tetchy and often snapped at her. His charm seemed to be kept for visiting friends when he would wow them with his good humour, jokes and fascinating conversation. Emily would watch silently, rarely interrupting or having her say. She realised that her essential character and personality were being overwhelmed and diminished by her ebullient husband. It suddenly dawned on her one day that she was turning into Seth's mother. She remembered the long-suffering look on her face and the bullying tone of her husband. Obviously, Seth and his father had much in common. Why had she not seen this before? Only when she was with her own girlfriends was she her old self, laughing and relaxing in a way she could not with her own husband.

Some days, he was a total delight. They would drive out into the country, visiting the villages and towns that surrounded Manchester. The countryside was stunning. They were so fortunate to be living in such a fabulous location, though the seemingly endless rain was something of a dampener. But when the weather promised no rain, even if not hot sunshine, they would dash to the car and take the opportunity to go exploring once again.

One such day, Seth wanted to go for a long drive and agreed to go to the stunning village of Robin Hood's Bay, which Emily had heard so much about. This beautiful village is nestled in a tiny bay on the east coast, famous for its steep streets and gorgeous winding alleyways leading down to the picturesque harbour. It was also renowned for its fabulous fish and chips! It would be a long drive so they set off early but it was a lovely run and by lunchtime, they were in close proximity to the village. Fish and chips beckoned. The signpost showed the way and Seth turned left, away from the Bay.

"What are you doing, Seth? The sign said the other way. We've come all this way. I don't understand."

He didn't answer, just kept driving up the coast towards the north, and Robin Hood's Bay receded into the distance.

"Why did you do that? Please answer me. Surely we should discuss this, not just ignore me" she cried.

Silence. No answer was forthcoming, and a couple of minutes later, he started chatting and joking as though nothing had transpired. His chatter flowed over her as she sat in mute misery not understanding what made his mind tick. Could he not understand his behaviour was bizarre and that it was affecting their relationship? He seemed to live in a different world to her own and she could not in any way comprehend the workings of his mind. She had also come to realise when he behaved like this that she could not push the matter further as there was an undercurrent of violence, even if nothing was verbally threatened. It was a look, a demeanour which made her shiver and feel scared. She was alone and cut off from her family and she longed for the life she had known. Was this the future? Once again, she buried her disquieting thoughts, too frightened to delve deeply. If she started to analyse her problems, where would it take her? There was seemingly no way out and she kept her mouth shut, yet again.

He eventually drove to another village on the coast, pretty enough but definitely not on a par with Robin Hood's Bay. They found a restaurant by the jetty and ate their fish and chips washed down with a glass of cider. Seth was lively and talked about all sorts but Emily sat eating her food in virtual silence as the water lapped its tiny waves onto the shoreline. The food tasted like sawdust to her but she managed to swallow most of it. Seth, as always, seemed impervious to her mood. They sauntered along the beach picking up shells and watching the boats and the gulls swooping down over the fishing boats landing their catches, shouting their demands in their raucous voices. It was such a lovely location but totally wasted on Emily who was trying desperately to work out what motivated her husband in his behaviour.

They drove back to Manchester, he still chatting and she in silence, hurt and bewildered. The day had been ruined, and it had started so well. If only she could understand. She had so wanted to go to the village, and Seth had known this and agreed and yet he had driven straight past without a word of explanation.

Emily made some supper and just slapped some food on the table. After they had eaten she asked him “do you want a hot drink?”

“Maybe I do and maybe I don’t” came the answer. What sort of answer was that, Emily wondered. But she made them each a cup of tea. Seth cleared the table and washed up, something he rarely did, still in high good humour. Emily went to watch a television programme and tried to empty her mind of the day’s events. She decided she would just go to bed and hope sleep would blot out the whole outing in her mind. Tomorrow would be a better day, wouldn’t it? She realised she needed a diversion in her life, which would be independent of her marriage. It would need some thought.

Emily set herself the task of finding the solution and came up with the notion of returning to an idea planted in her head by her college friend Daisy, and repeated by Harriet, and that would be to join a choir. She began to investigate what was available locally to her and found a community choir close to her local shops, which met every Tuesday evening. The choir Harriet attended was further away, so she decided against that one. This one sounded ideal. She called the number in the advert, spoke to the choirmaster who had answered the phone and arranged to have a try-out the following week. He had asked her a number of questions about her previous experience singing in choirs, and she told him she had none and couldn't sight read. That's not a problem, he told her and he was sure she would pick things up quickly. Such a relief! Emily was delighted and excited. She had decided that she had to find an outlet for her personality that would take her out of the house and the toxic atmosphere that was developing, although she was the only one who apparently felt it. Maybe she was imagining it, and really all was well in her life?

The choir members proved to be friendly and outgoing, gathering round her with a barrage of questions. It was lovely to be known just for herself with no-one aware of her circumstances. She told them she thought she was a soprano. The choirmaster, called Martin, came up to welcome her. "We sing a cross-section of songs. Sight reading isn't necessary, just the ability to sing in tune and you can relax – there's no audition!"

"Thank goodness," she smiled back at him. He gave her copies of the sheet music and found her a place to sit and the warm-up began. Then it was into the songs.

There was much laughter, no chit-chat, just the sheer joy of singing, opening her mouth wide and letting rip! Some of the music she already knew as they were songs she had been brought up with, heard on the radio in her youth and also a selection from the shows. It would be a steep learning curve to catch up, but well worth the effort. The choir did perform in public and held an annual concert in a hall locally where family, friends and interested members of the public could hear them. In addition, she was told, they would sometimes perform in care homes or in shopping centres, especially around Christmas time. There were several months to go to the next concert and Emily knew she had a lot of practising to do but it would be such fun.

It was all new to her, obviously, but after the warm-up, when their voices were exercised and ready to go, they launched into the first song, which was from Fiddler on the Roof, one of her favourite musicals. She certainly knew the tune but they sang in parts so, as she was not completely sure where to come in. She watched the girl next to her and when she saw her take a deep breath, knew it was time to make an entrance. This worked well, and looking at the music, some of the theory she had learned years ago began to come back to her. She realised suddenly that she was having such fun. This was going to be a lifesaver for her. She settled into enjoying herself and during the break, people came up to her and started to chat. They were so welcoming. Leaving the rehearsal hall that evening she was aware she was smiling broadly and surrounded by like-minded people and felt a happiness that had not been part of her life for many a long day. This was definitely something to enjoy each week and became a highlight in her life.

Emily opened their front door, almost delirious with happiness at how her evening had turned out, and she spilled out her experience in a torrent of words, singing snatches of the tunes which were buzzing around in her mind. Seth laughed at her enthusiasm and told her he was so delighted that she had discovered this new outlet and couldn't wait to go to the concert. He was so loving and warm, and Emily glowed under his attention.

Another bonus was that they appeared to have found a house to buy. It was in Didsbury, which had excellent transport links to central Manchester and so convenient for Emily's school and Seth's library. It was a lovely area with a wide variety of houses, parks and a village atmosphere with cafes, restaurants and shops. The street the house was located in was lined with flowering trees which would be covered in blossom in the spring. They were so lucky to have found this property. It was a three-bedroomed, semi-detached property built between the two World Wars with a pretty, south-facing garden, very typical of the area. The two reception rooms were a good size although the kitchen was smallish but it was entirely adequate and was fully fitted with fairly new, up-to-date units. The main bedroom was generous and even the smallest bedroom was not a bad size, certainly good enough for a single guest or eventually a baby's first bedroom. It even had a garage attached. The owners were moving abroad and needed a quick sale, so they accepted the moderate offer from Seth and Emily, who were able to move quickly with the legalities. It was an excellent buy and Emily asked their solicitor to get the deeds sorted fast. Once again, Seth was 'too busy' to get involved in the buying process and left his wife to deal with all the paperwork. She also arranged the mortgage and the survey. The house would be theirs in under a month with a rapid completion date. They were all set to move now.

"Can you take the day off next Wednesday?" Emily asked Seth. "I've got time off because it's half-term but I really need your help with the move. I don't think I can manage on my own. It will be too problematic coping with this flat and ensuring everything arrives safely at the new house and put in the right rooms. I can't be in two places at once."

"That's impossible. We're short-staffed as it is. I'm sure you'll manage. You always do" he snapped dismissively.

"I know you have problems at work but surely they will understand your need for a day off. You can take it out of your holiday allowance. I really will need help" Emily retorted.

Seth ignored her and walked out of the room. Emily stared after his retreating back and sat down slowly on the sofa, her head in her hands, willing herself not to let the tears come. All her husband did within the marriage, she realised, was to take. He put nothing in. She paid the bulk of the bills from their joint bank account but she saw sums disappearing from it, which left the balance dangerously low. What was he spending it on? When she asked, all she got was her head snapped off for her pains. He did nothing in the way of shopping and cleaning even though she worked full time. She also saw to all the administration of running their lives and what was she getting back? Sex, that was all. Thank goodness they had no children to add to the mix.

Emily realised she was on her own with the move and would have to somehow manage. She always did manage in the end, but she should not have to. After all, she was married. It was supposed to be a partnership, a sharing of everything that was necessary. This definitely was not her reality.

A few minutes later he stuck his head round the door with a big grin on his face.

"I forgot to tell you. I've invited some of our friends over on Saturday night to the new house to check it out. It will be fun, won't it?"

"Are you joking?" Emily shouted, "We're only moving on Wednesday. That's so thoughtless of you. How can we entertain people just a couple of days later? You'll have to phone and cancel."

"It'll be fine. Don't get your knickers in a twist. We'll just buy in food and they can help us to sort things out. But you're so capable, I know everything will be sorted by then." He smiled and came over to give her a quick hug. She heard the front door shut, and sitting alone she contemplated her situation. Two years into marriage and, unhappiness thrust its load on her head, through her entire body and deep into her psyche.

She sat unmoving like this for the better part of an hour, unable to bestir herself or think clearly. What on earth could she do and how to move forward? She needed help and advice but whom could she turn to? There was virtually no help for people like her. Domestic abuse was virtually ignored in this country. The police were not interested; doctors and church leaders just told you to accept the inevitable and get on with it. She had read an article that some woman was trying to set up shelters for battered wives, but it was just a tiny glimmer of light in a deep black hole of violence and misery.

Was she alone in feeling like this? It seemed unlikely to her. But she had no idea where to turn or how to deal with the situation. She was frightened and alone, not knowing what to do. Talking to her parents was not an option, nor to her friends. They all considered she had a perfect life, a handsome, charming husband, a beautiful home and a burgeoning career. How could she disabuse them. She, alone, had determined to go into this marriage but now she could see how completely unrealistic she had been. She had let her heart rule her head, she realised, blocking out and ignoring all the warning signs. Maybe this was her new 'normal'. Maybe all marriages were like this, including that of her parents. Who knew what was actually happening behind closed doors?

Emily knew nothing of the world of abused women. Her life experiences totally precluded any knowledge of such a lifestyle. Violence against a partner she knew was abuse, but what else constituted abuse, she wondered. She had no idea and there was no help out there, or none that she knew of. She would just have to battle it out and hope she could survive the insidious drip-drip of insults and pettiness which were becoming an almost daily occurrence. She didn't have a clue. That was the problem, nobody said anything. She could not be alone but she had no idea how to access any information. The papers regularly reported about women who were killed by their partners, and everybody wrung their hands and said they had had no idea what had been going on. Her married friends seemed happy and content, but then so did she in public. At least she had her singing, something to revel in. She pulled herself upright, straightened her back and went to pack more boxes.

CHAPTER 16

The day of the move proved to be sunny and warm. Emily woke up at the crack of dawn after a fitful night of poor sleep, dreaming of disasters, breakages and other horrendous things that could go wrong with the move and dreading having to deal with it all on her own. This should not have been the case and she was resentful and angry at the situation. She hated what she was becoming, knowing she was often showing the world a surly face and giving the appearance of a misery-guts. This was so unlike the person she had been in a previous life, before marriage, when she had always had a ready smile and was so quick to laugh. That person had completely disappeared, and she missed her.

She made herself a cup of coffee, hoping the caffeine would revive her. Seth was moving about the bedroom and came into the kitchen, gave her a kiss and a hug and disappeared off to work early, obviously having decided to keep a low profile and not to become the object of Emily's ire. The removal men would be arriving shortly and she had to sort out the last bits of packing, just personal things, plus the all-important kettle and mugs. The knock came on the door, the men came in, and the removal began.

The men walked in the door, behind Emily, who had the key. She was so excited to turn this wonderful symbol of ownership in the door of her very own property! "First things first" she said, "I'll find the kettle and make a brew." Tea downed, biscuits scoffed, the men set to with impressive speed and efficiency and made the whole procedure appear as simple as possible. Arriving at the house, they put the labelled boxes in the appropriate rooms, drank more tea, ate the remaining biscuits and went off having pocketed the hefty tip she gave them. Emily sat on the sofa, gave a contented sigh and contemplated where to start. The pile of boxes looked like an impenetrable mountain and she decided to begin in the kitchen.

By mid-afternoon, nearly all the boxes had been emptied, cupboards and wardrobes filled, and the furniture arranged. She felt like an octopus with so many limbs piling cutlery, crockery and clothes into drawers and cupboards. She was exhausted. Her back ached as she sat on a kitchen chair with a restorative cup of tea yet with a smug feeling of a job well done. Seth had certainly got away lightly, she thought. He would come home, and their new home would be tidy, warm and welcoming, but she certainly was not going to make a meal. He could take her out, that was for sure.

Seth arrived home with a conciliatory bunch of flowers, which looked as though they came from the local garage forecourt. "I told you it would not be a big job," he stated smugly, looking round their new home. "I don't know why you had to make such a fuss about me not taking the day off." He put his arms around her and held her tight. Emily wanted to wriggle out of his way but then decided not to make an issue of things. He might have got away with his behaviour, but she certainly would not forget his treatment of her and total disregard for her as a wife, an individual and a life partner.

"But you are taking me out to dinner and somewhere nice. You're not getting away with it altogether and you owe me big time. And next time we move, I definitely will not be doing it all by myself. You really need to pull your weight more."

"That's a deal" he answered cheerfully. He was always quick to say what she wanted to hear. He fetched Emily's coat, ready to go out to find a restaurant in their new area.

They both loved their new home. They met the neighbours, who seemed congenial and pleasant and started to discover the neighbourhood and what it had to offer. There were some lovely boutiques and also trendy cafes and restaurants, and they decided they would try them all out one by one, mainly one night a week, until they found their favourite. The bus stop was nearby and was on a direct route to Emily's work, though Seth would need to change, but that would not be a big problem. All in all, they were both delighted with the decision they had made to move to the locality and even Seth seemed to be making more of an effort. Emily was delighted and started to relax and feel more hopeful for the future. Maybe their new home would be the making of their marriage.

Life continued on an even keel with only an occasional snide remark from Seth. Emily began to relax, and really enjoyed her teaching job at the school, but the highlight of her week was definitely Tuesday evening at choir practice. The concert was fast approaching, a hall booked, Martin told them and tickets would be going to be available to buy. The hall held about 200 people apparently and most of the audience would constitute family and friends of the singers. Rehearsals took on an intensity that increased as the due date approached, and finally, it arrived.

Seth had been very encouraging with her singing and kept telling her how much he was looking forward to the concert. He was so proud of her and her lovely soprano voice, and the programme sounded varied and fun. Emily would sing the songs at home, while cleaning or doing the washing up, repeating the difficult bits of descant till she had perfected them. She definitely was now ready for the big event. She would leave for the concert earlier in the day as the singers would have to become used to the hall, rehearse their entry and know where to stand. Seth would arrive just before the concert was due to begin.

Emily arrived at the hall dressed in a black skirt and top as instructed. The men were to wear black trousers, white shirts and a light blue tie, and the ladies had matching long blue scarves to drape around their necks. Music was held in a black ring binder. They looked smart and professional. Emily, being so small, had a position in the front row of three with taller people in the back.

The audience arrived, and the volume of chatter rose, and then Martin took his place on the podium, raised his baton and smiled encouragingly at the singers. They began with the first medley from recent shows and they were off! Everybody knew the songs well and Emily was amused to see the audience mouthing the words but just falling short of actually joining in. The first half ended, and she mingled with the other choristers and introduced Seth to her friends, drinking the tea on offer, accompanied by home-made cakes and biscuits, then returned to her place, and the second half began. They finished with an enthusiastic rendering of the Beatles number I Want to Hold Your Hand. As the last note died away, there was loud clapping and cheering from one and all. It had gone brilliantly. The odd mistake had crept in, certainly, but nobody would have noticed and no errors of any consequence. Emily felt euphoric. Seldom had she had such an adrenaline rush. Now she understood why so many wanted to go on the stage.

"What did you think? Wasn't it brilliant Seth."

"You were amazing, and I loved the selection. It was such a well-balanced programme and really fun" he answered. "I must go and congratulate Martin."

Martin had a crowd around him and Seth tapped him on the shoulder. "Did you enjoy it?" he smilingly asked Seth.

"What a waste of an evening" Seth started. "I don't know why you bother with this lot. It was a complete waste of time. You really should find yourself another profession. And to think I actually paid good money to listen to this fucking crap."

There was a stunned silence from everyone within earshot. What was going on? This could not be for real. Who on earth would be so nasty and vicious? Emily stood rooted to the spot, her face beetroot red with embarrassment and sheer horror. This was her husband being so obnoxious. Why was he doing this? She turned and ran from the room, blinded by the tears coursing down her cheeks, and into the street. She stood in the cold, not even noticing that she didn't have a coat. He had ruined everything. Gone was her greatest happiness. This had to be the end of her choir involvement. She certainly could never return or hold her head up again in their company. Was that Seth's aim, she asked herself?

The next thing an arm went round her. "Let's go home" a cheerful Seth said, apparently very pleased with himself and a job well done. She let herself be steered to the car, trying not to touch him and totally unable to say a word. She had experienced such joy that evening. Was that the problem? Was Seth jealous? But why did he have to act so callously and cruelly? Why not just punish her? Why involve the others, what had they ever done to harm him? She just couldn't think. She had never experienced anything like this in her entire life. It was all so confusing and the hurt she felt ran so deep, like a dagger into her very essence, flooding her with pain which was destroying her from within. She had no idea how she would move on from this.

Before the concert, Seth had been enthusiastic about going to hear her sing. He had encouraged her and told family and friends how marvellous she was and yet here she was now, sitting in the car with a man who had carefully and systematically planned to destroy and humiliate her in front of her peers. What was his motivation, and did he not see the relationship between cause and effect? He declared his undying love for her but could not perceive that he was doing everything in his power to smash it to pieces. And that was the problem. She still loved him, and so she sublimated his behaviour deep into her innermost being, unable to face the truth of what was occurring. Emily consciously refused to face reality. Once again she decided not to think matters through. She knew, deep down, that this was what she needed to do but once more came to the conclusion that she was exaggerating the situation. What really stunned Emily above all else was that he seemed so pleased with himself, smug even, at a job well done. This was certainly planned, she was shocked to realise. She buried her misgivings and horror.

Even now, after such disgusting behaviour, she made excuses for him. She did not blame herself at all as she had enough awareness to know that this was not her fault. The culpability was all his. She appreciated that she was not perfect but nor was anyone, and she certainly did not deserve the actions being meted out to her. In some ways she understood that this was not what a marriage or relationship should be but was unwilling to sit down, analyse and come to the conclusion that she should not stay in such a toxic partnership. She appreciated she could not let herself go down that road. Seth was chatting and laughing as he always did after abusing her and she felt herself, once again, softening towards him. His manipulation was complete and he certainly knew that he had won the day.

They arrived back at the house, Emily quiet and quiescent. Seth was voluble and triumphant. They went up, undressed and made ready for bed. Emily turned her back on Seth, but he pulled her roughly towards him. His touch felt obnoxious to her. She struggled and shouted at him, "leave me alone," but he would not take 'no' for an answer. He grabbed her by the hair and kissed her roughly, bruising her mouth and biting her neck hard. He then ignored her cries and threw her onto her back on the bed, and thrust himself into her with no preparation, forcing her down into the mattress and using his whole weight against her. He whispered words of love into her ear as she struggled beneath him. The words sickened her. How could he use such terms while abusing her both physically and emotionally? She had no control. Totally beaten, she gave up the fight. Her humanity had vanished, and she had become an object with no rights and no personality – just a piece of meat and a possession for him to control and own. She wept quietly as he finished with her. He turned his back and was immediately asleep. It was rape, again. He had won again.

CHAPTER 17

Emily looked in the mirror and was shocked at the damage to her face and body. Her mouth was bruised and sore, and she had a huge hickey where he had bitten her hard on the neck. Her shoulders were bruised, all shades of purple through to black, and even her breasts were sore where he had grabbed her and twisted her nipples. She was a mess. The evidence would have to go. She took out her make-up bag, found the concealer and set to. Covering up the evidence was becoming routine to her. The damage to her neck would be hidden by a polo neck top plus a scarf for added protection. Luckily, it was winter. Nothing could be done about the all-over soreness. That would just have to wear off, and she decided on some paracetamol to deaden the pain. She swallowed two of the pills with a drink of water and hoped for the best.

She showered, flinching as the shards of water pierced her skin, but she scrubbed herself as best she could to wash away his violence and her violation. Emily felt revolting and revolted. He was her husband. He declared over and over how much he loved her, how much she meant to him and yet he treated her worse than a whipped dog. But she did not let the thoughts stay with her, nor did she follow them to a conclusion. As usual, she buried the horror deep in her very being, unwilling to face what her life had become. She also knew well how he would be this morning.

And so it was. He had come downstairs and prepared breakfast, whistling as he laid the table and smiling at her with not a hint of irony. This should have been amazing to her, but of course, it wasn't. He seemed like a split personality, as though each half was unaware of the other. A pathological liar, she knew this of him. Did he lie to himself also about his behaviour to her? Did he truly believe that he was being a true, loving husband? She could not work it out and, once more, just gave up through total exhaustion.

Emily sat at the table, unable to swallow the food put in front of her. The hot coffee made her wince when it touched her damaged mouth. Seth did not seem to notice her lack of appetite or her pain. He chattered on about what they should do that day. He never mentioned the concert at all. It was as if it had never occurred. They would go to the art gallery and see the exhibition that was on there. "I've heard it's really good. I know you will love it. The Post-Impressionists are your favourites, aren't they" he said. "Maybe we can go to that new café afterwards that everybody is talking about. I'd really like to try it out. I'm sure Harriet and David would like to join us. I'll go and give them a call, and they can meet us there. Go and fetch your coat, and we'll be off."

Her body had stiffened up overnight and she could barely get her arms into the sleeves of the coat. Seth saw her struggling but made no comment as to the reason for her problem but helped her on with it. There was no sympathy and certainly no apology or regret at what he had done to her. There was no word of explanation. Nothing, in fact. She walked silently to the car while he sat in the driver's seat and drove them to the centre of Manchester and the art gallery. Another ordinary day had begun.

Harriet and David were waiting for them by the entrance. They seemed excited and were obviously longing to impart some news and were oblivious that Emily was so quiet and withdrawn.

"I'm pregnant" Harriet blurted out. "Isn't that the most amazing news? We couldn't wait to tell you. I'm due in June and our parents are so excited at the thought of a grandchild to spoil. It's really scary though" she continued.

"I can't believe I'm going to be a dad" David cut in. "It's such a responsibility. I just hope I'm up to it and don't make a mess of fatherhood."

"Of course you won't, silly. You'll be an amazing father," his wife said, looking at him with such adoration and pride that made Emily feel sick inside with envy. She was delighted for her friend and gave her a huge cuddle, David too, but she couldn't deal with the hurt inside that she, too, did not have this total love from her husband. How would he be as a father? It made her tremble to even consider it. Would his abuse extend to his children? She could not bear to contemplate an innocent child – her child – suffering at the hands of its own father. Getting pregnant was surely out of the question. That was definite.

The whole, horrible incident was forgotten, by Seth anyway. Emily, as usual, said nothing and carried on regardless. Term started, and she quickly got back into the swing of the school day. She had been given the sixth form to teach their 'A' level history class, which was challenging and exciting. They would be covering the Tudor period, which delighted Emily as she could concentrate on her favourite monarch, Elizabeth I. Who could not admire this lady who controlled and manipulated her Court, the country and the world beyond by dint of her personality and amazing brain. Emily wished she had a fraction of the gumption of Elizabeth and envied her strength of character. Elizabeth would never have found herself in the ghastly situation in which Emily was embroiled. It was ironic that she was jealous of someone who had died over four hundred years previously!

Home was relatively peaceful, though Seth seemed to be finding more and more ways to psychologically abuse her. He had back-handed her several times now. He was verbally abusive and hypercritical, insulting and humiliating her for no reason except for his own apparent amusement. They would lie in bed while she had to listen to a list of her many failings, which were extremely varied, from what she gave him to eat to her sense of humour (or lack of it) and her social skills. Some were petty but some were complicated and obviously planned.

Sunday morning dawned miserable and wet. She, therefore, decided to do the household task she most abhorred, washing the kitchen floor. The bucket was filled with hot, soapy water, and she started to mop the grubby floor. It was raining with a steady soggy drizzle and she noticed that Seth had gone out into the garden. What was that about, she wondered. She watched him through the patio doors as he trampled in the flowerbeds, the rain steadily soaking him. She soon found out. He came back into the kitchen, trailing water, his shoes covered in mud and trampled all over the newly-washed floors making sure he covered the whole kitchen. Emily stood watching, horrified. What next, she thought to herself.

"I've just washed that floor" she said.

"So wash it again" he replied and walked out of the room leaving a sea of filthy footprints and muddy earth behind him. She did.

How did he think these things up, she asked herself. What was his thinking? His behaviour was definitely spiralling out of control, worsening every day. This could not continue, and the marriage would have to come to an end. It was a total farce. Immediately after he would be Mr Charming and make an effort to bring her round with his silver tongue, which he employed to good effect.

Emily began to plan in her mind how to move forward. She now suddenly appreciated that this marriage must end. A red line had been crossed, and the partnership had to be terminated. There was no alternative. She would need to confide in her parents, who were totally unaware of her situation and her misery. They were down in London, she in Manchester, and so they were not in a position to view her everyday mood. When she saw them, it was only for a couple of days at a time, and she gave the appearance of being upbeat and happy. Nor could she get out of her mind that they had had deep reservations about Seth from the outset and guessed that these doubts had not gone away from the odd remark her mother and father let slip. Emily was so ashamed at her lack of judgment in having chosen to marry such a flawed personality, and she had been too embarrassed to confide in her parents or even in her closest friend, Suzanne, who had visited the previous weekend.

That was also strange, she now realised. Seth had always liked Suzanne. He would sing her praises at the drop of a hat, welcomed her when she visited and talked positively about her. He considered her warm and empathetic, clever and sassy, or so he had always said. Since Suzanne had left a few days before, Seth had been cutting and nasty every time Suzanne's name cropped up. What was going on and why the change of heart? Emily was puzzled and also miserable at the thought that her deep friendship with Suzanne was in jeopardy. She put the thought to one side for now.

A solicitor would have to be consulted, as well as finances, to work out. They owned a house between them but the entire amount of the very substantial deposit and the purchase of the contents had come from her family's funding. How would that affect the division of effects? Why should Seth get half? That did not seem fair at all. She would definitely have to sit down with her parents who knew so much more than she did and also had friends who could advise her before she actually consulted a solicitor.

She sat down in the living room and took out her diary. She would go down to London to speak with her parents. It was not a conversation to have over the phone so she needed to find a few clear days when she could travel down. The half-term break would be a good time to go, and she checked the dates so she could let her parents know. She was thumbing through her diary when she froze with horror. She rapidly checked again and again, obsessively. Her period was five days late. This never happened. She was like clockwork. Surely it couldn't be. A wave of depression tore through her, and she gasped, the breath refusing to come and a tight compression in her chest as she realised the implications.

Seth would not let her go on the pill, saying not enough was known of its long-term consequences, but they were both meticulous in using protection when they had sex. She no longer thought of it as 'making love'. This was not a marriage of mutual affection and devotion. She accepted having sex with Seth. It was the only time in their shared existence when he was considerate and thoughtful, and she, too, had needs. He fulfilled those requirements.

Emily tried to think back to when they had maybe been remiss, and in a flash, she recalled the night of the ghastly concert and Seth forcing himself on her. She now remembered that contraception had been the last thing on her mind and none had been used. That had to be the answer. Now she might be pregnant as a result of an act which could only be termed 'rape'. Mind you, society did not recognise rape possible within marriage. A husband could do what he liked, with the law totally disregarding the violence implied in the act. She was scuppered.

The only way to get confirmation of her condition would be to make an appointment with her doctor. She would phone the surgery first thing in the morning and certainly had no intention of saying anything to Seth as yet, as she needed time to think things through and decide what to do. In fact, if a test proved positive, she would have to re-assess her whole situation even to decide if she would proceed with the pregnancy. Abortion had been legal for six or seven years now, but could she go down that road? She thought not, and on what grounds would she manage to have a termination? This was her child, after all, and she would love it dearly, but how would she manage as a single mother with little practical help or support?

The following morning, first thing, Emily waited for Seth to leave the house, made the call and managed to get a cancellation, thank goodness, and immediately phoned the school to say she would be a few minutes late as she had an early doctor's appointment. She left the house with her small container with her urine sample wrapped up carefully and placed in the bottom of her bag. The wait was only a few minutes before being called into the surgery, where she told the doctor that her period was late and she had brought a sample for testing. This would have to be sent away and she now had an agonising few days' wait for the results to come through. The doctor had congratulated her, but she found it difficult to respond. He gave her a long, hard look, but she said nothing further.

The week passed so slowly. Emily tried hard not to think of what might be, and it was difficult concentrating in class and not let anything slip at home. Seth was still moderately acceptable in his behaviour towards her, though he was working long hours at the library as they were short-staffed. It did mean he was paid overtime, however, though she noted that it did not seem to be reflected in the balance in their joint bank account. Finally, after an agonising wait, she was given an appointment with the doctor, to receive her results.

CHAPTER 18

They were positive.

What was she to do? Emily had finally decided to apply for a divorce, and now the whole situation had been turned upside down. Society still deemed divorce unacceptable in the early 1970s. There was a stigma attached to it despite the easing of the rules governing divorce, which made the whole process simpler. Nevertheless, it was considered a last resort, but her misery and unhappiness were so overwhelming she had decided to go ahead. Being a divorcee as a single woman was problematic. Being a divorcee with a baby in tow was a completely different scenario.

Judges still veered in favour of the man. Despite suffering abuse, in many cases, the wife was not believed, and she was accordingly penalised in the divorce settlement as being 'unreasonable.' Emily was also pretty certain that Seth would not pay maintenance for her and their child. He would undertake to do so, but the reality would be a different matter altogether. He did not like to part with his money and often refused to pay bills that he had run up, just ignoring them. Emily would quietly pay them. He was not a man of honour or high ethics, as his wife had found out to her cost. When first married, he had ignored bills such as the phone or electricity, and the service would be cut off. Emily had decided to take over the finances to ensure a smooth ride through domestic financial life. She was sure that maintenance for his child would not materialise after the first couple of payments, and she would have to spend much time, energy and money fighting him through the Courts for the next 18 years. His charm was one hundred percent superficial, just rolled out when he wanted to get someone onside.

She needed time and space to mull the matter over and would say nothing to Seth in the meantime. Though very soon, he would realise that she was not experiencing her period and so decided she would have to pretend in order to give her breathing space. Emily was not a devious person, and it did not sit comfortably with her pretending something that was not true, but there was no alternative for the time being.

It was hard to maintain a silence. Emily was naturally open and chatty and hated to keep such a momentous secret to herself. She wanted to shout her news from the rooftops. She longed for this baby, but not with such a husband in tow. What sort of father would he make with his continual, pathological lying, violence and instability? She could not rely on him for anything. He seemed to be making no effort to better himself in his employment, and there had been no promotions or salary rises. How could she work full time and care for a child if he would not do his fair share of the household chores or provide enough money to pay for child care?

On the other hand, if she were a single parent, how would she manage alone with working and looking after her baby? The only way to do so was to move back down to London to be close to her parents whom she was sure would support her both financially and with bringing up her child. Emily realised that a termination was not on the cards. This was her child and she would give it life, nurture and love it with all her might. On that score, she was decided. Now, she would also have to consider how Seth would react when he discovered she was pregnant with his child. They had never really discussed starting a family and she didn't know his feelings on the subject. She had never investigated this aspect of his character as the abuse had started so early in the marriage that she had suppressed all thoughts of having children. This was frightening, and she really needed someone to act as a sounding board and realised she would have to go down to London and talk with her parents. She badly needed their love and support to see her through this enormously vital stage in her life.

Emily did her best to maintain her work standards at the school. Luckily, the pupils helped her take her mind off her problems, at least for a few hours, during the day. She was a popular teacher; the girls wanted to learn, and she managed to keep her thoughts to herself and well away from Harriet when they were in the staff room together. Sometimes, Harriet gave her a long, thoughtful look and seemed about to start a conversation about something that worried her but she never actually managed to get the words out. Emily suspected that Harriet believed something might be wrong so she ensured that the two friends were not ensconced alone together for long periods at a time. Emily was not yet ready to divulge her pregnancy just as Harriet's waistline was expanding with her own.

Fortunately, though still very early days, Emily was not suffering any morning sickness. That would really be difficult to hide. Sometimes feeling a bit queasy, she managed to hide it from Seth. She soon worked out which food items were the triggers and avoided them, only cooking dishes that would not bother her. Taking meat out of the oven was the worst as the smell wafted up to overwhelm her. She stuck to chicken and fish, which were not so problematic. She wanted to buy some time whilst she prepared the ground for the next step.

Paradoxically, Seth was going through a 'be nice to Emily' phase. She had no idea what had caused this change in his attitude, but experience had taught her that this stage was purely temporary. Having no idea how long it would last it, at least it gave her some extra time before a confrontation would be inevitable. He was still coming up with his ridiculous sayings whenever she asked him a direct question, particularly when she asked him if he wanted something such as a drink. 'Maybe I do, and maybe I don't,' he would always reply. What did that mean? Another one that he trotted out with extreme regularity when she asked him where he was going was 'out and about' or a variation was 'here and there'.

"What about having some people over for dinner soon? We haven't done any entertaining for a while and I really would love some of your fancy cooking. You make the best pastry of anyone," he said. "We could make a date for next week if you want. Make a list of who you want to invite, and I'll phone round. While I do that, you can think up a menu of what you could make."

"We could do, but I would need some help with the shopping and preparation," Emily mused. "You seem to have so many late shifts at the library. You will have to let me know what date suits you so that you could be home in plenty of time. I think a weekend night would be best, don't you?"

"That would be the easiest, and then there would be no conflict with work," he replied.

This would help take her mind off her body and keep Seth's mind off her, she thought. She took out her address book and sat down to make a list of whom to invite.

Three couples were invited, so there would be eight round the table. Harriet and David were included in the list and Harriet would be well on in her pregnancy. There were certain foodstuffs she could not tolerate at the moment. Emily would need to check with her friend before finalising her menu. Seth had also invited a couple whom Emily had never encountered but had heard him talk about. The wife, Anna, worked with him at the library, and he told her she was bright and good fun, although he had not yet met her husband. Emily had never met any of his colleagues at the library so she was looking forward to getting to know at least one of them. The dinner would be on Saturday night.

The day arrived and Emily rose early to start her cooking. Seth left the house to go to the shops to buy all the ingredients for the food, plus choosing wine to go with the meal. Emily rolled up her sleeves and got cracking, systematically working through her list until most of the work was completed. She then whizzed round with the vacuum cleaner and a duster, tidied errant objects and newspapers and started laying the table. She found a pretty tablecloth which she spread out and placed a small posy of flowers in the middle of the table. Cutlery, clean wine glasses and napkins followed and all was done. She stood back to study her handiwork and admitted to herself that it all looked lovely and very welcoming. She was very satisfied with her efforts and looked forward to a joyful evening with good company and excellent food. Emily loved entertaining. It was a great deal of work but well worth the effort.

Their first visitors arrived right on time, quickly followed by Harriet and David. Harriet looked well and flourishing, her bump preceding her into the room, where she collapsed with a big sigh into the armchair.

"I know it will be well worth the effort and the discomfort when the baby arrives," she said "but I have to say that I can't wait for him or her to arrive. Though, of course, then the real work will start: sleepless nights, crying, and baby sick. We can't wait, though. I don't know who is more excited – us or our parents. This is a first grandchild for both sets of parents."

"They will spoil the baby rotten, won't they? And we will have to deal with the fallout," David continued. "But it's so exciting. I've always wanted to be a dad."

"I don't know," Seth butted in. "Won't it mean a total change in your lifestyle? No going out when you want, money going out constantly for the baby's needs. And it only gets worse as they get older. I think we will wait a while before we go down that route. Give us a few years to enjoy ourselves without the responsibilities of parenthood."

Emily decided not to make any comment but made the excuse that she needed to see how the food was progressing in the kitchen. She opened the oven carefully so as not to get a blast of cooking smells and thought about what Seth had said. He obviously had no idea about her condition, and it was early days yet. However, once she started to show and her figure changed then she would have to come clean and also find an explanation for not telling him sooner. She would cross that bridge when she came to it.

Life was certainly getting more and more complicated, and she had to make her move pretty soon.

The friend from the library, Anna, was a pretty girl and seemed bright, just as Seth had said. The husband, who was called Alan, looked at her adoringly and kept a protective arm round her as they came into the living room and they were introduced. Everybody was soon happily chatting, and presently, they went into the dining room where everyone oohed and aahed over the table. Seth told everyone where to sit. He had Anna to his right and David to his other side, and Emily brought in the starter.

The evening progressed happily. The food kept coming, and the wine flowed, leading to much laughter and rising noise levels. The evening was a success. Seth was the perfect host, charming, witty and amusing, telling funny anecdotes about people in the library, both staff and users. Their guests loved it, gazing at him raptly with smiles on their faces as he kept them amused. He was at his best, and Emily watched him, wondering why he was not like this all the time. Why was he such a Jekyll and Hyde personality, she wondered sadly, never consistent and always so unpredictable. All, except herself, thought he was wonderful.

The evening came to an end in the early hours, and their guests gathered up their coats and other bits and pieces, said their goodbyes with many thanks for a wonderful evening, and made their way into the night. Emily and Seth were left alone to look at the debris on the table and the dirty glasses littering the living room.

"What did you think of Anna and her husband?" Seth asked as he took another load of dirty plates into the kitchen. "She's nice, isn't she? And I liked her husband. It's the first time I've met him. They seem well suited."

"You were very attentive to her" Emily commented, "certainly being very conscientious in your host duties to her."

"Well, it was her first visit to us and I didn't want her to feel left out. She might have felt a bit overwhelmed at first with all these new people and she is rather shy."

"Do you want a hot drink" she asked. "Maybe I do, and maybe I don't" was the usual answer. Emily decided enough was enough. She made herself a cup of tea and sat down with it in the armchair. "I thought you were making me one," he said. "You couldn't seem to make up your mind" was her rejoinder, "so I decided that you obviously didn't. Maybe you should give a straight answer when asked a simple question." Why had it taken her so long to call his bluff? It was time she became more proactive and not be such a shrinking violet. Maybe she should take a leaf out of Elizabeth I's book. Now, there was an idea to think about!

Emily looked at him thoughtfully but decided not to continue with this conversation. She went to sort things out in the kitchen and let the matter drop, but she had a strange feeling about the evening. She wasn't exactly sure what had disconcerted her, but something surely had. She would keep her ears and eyes open and watch any developments very carefully.

CHAPTER 19

Sunday morning Seth went out to buy the newspaper and Emily took the opportunity to phone her parents.

"Mum, are you around this weekend? I really want to come down and visit you. There's something really important I want to discuss with you" she started.

"What's going on? Are you all right? You don't sound it. Please tell me a bit more."

"I can't discuss it on the phone. I need to see you face to face." By now Emily was on the verge of tears. It was so hard not to get emotional and she didn't want to upset her mother but knew she was not succeeding.

"We did have plans, but I'll cancel them. You're really worrying me now. Are you coming by yourself, or with Seth?"

"Definitely by myself. He doesn't know I'm planning to visit you so please don't tell him. Please" she pleaded.

"Of course not, if that's what you want. Anyway he never calls us so there's no reason for us to speak to him. Now you really have me very worried. You sound extremely upset." They pressed her for details but she would not say anything further. She would let them know when she saw them. She would also have to think up an excuse to tell Seth why she was going down to London without him but she would think of something. She disconnected but could hear the worry in her parents' voices. They would be even more anxious when she told them what she had in mind. Seth would not be told of her plans until later in the week which would reduce the pressure on her but she knew he would not be happy about her leaving for the weekend by herself.

They spent the day quietly after the excesses of the previous evening. They worked their way through all the sections of the bulky Sunday paper. Emily had a pile of marking to do so she settled down to get that under way while Seth pottered around the house and garden making minor repairs and catching up on odd jobs. This was not like him at all and Emily watched all this effort, somewhat bemused. Usually she did all the repairs, even changing light bulbs. Seth would say he would do the jobs but never actually did anything. Emily would ask him twice, he would agree to fix things but she always finished up doing them herself. His word meant zero, she had quickly learned. He would promise the world but deliver nothing. She would bang in nails, glue things together, paint walls and unblock sinks. She had become quite handy around the house as a result. Maybe when she had divorced him she could earn extra money as a handyman/woman? She certainly had plenty of experience by now.

Emily booked the train to leave after school finished on Friday to return late on Sunday. She would only need clothes for a couple of days so would only take a weekend bag which could be taken to school with her to go straight to the station. By Wednesday she had still not plucked up the courage to tell Seth that she was going away. This really brought home to her the realisation that life should not be like this. It was unacceptable to be so scared of her husband and life partner to the extent that she could not tell him that she was going to visit her parents. A marriage should not be this way. It should be a true partnership. Of course, if that had been the case for her then she would not have needed to run to her parents to plan her future when she was divorced. The irony was not lost on her.

There was a film Seth wanted to see. He loved violent films, where dozens of people were killed or maimed in the first two minutes. Emily hated this gratuitous violence and had soon realised that they never went to the cinema to see something she wanted to see. It was always his choice. In fact, it suddenly dawned her, they never did or went anywhere she wanted. She remembered the Robin Hood's Bay fiasco. He was still on 'a be nice to Emily' period so she decided to accede and off they went after supper.

The film was exactly as Emily had anticipated. His take on films was that violence was paramount. There had to be death and destruction in a non-stop orgy of misery and viciousness. Without these elements then it was deemed a lousy film. This movie fitted the bill to perfection. It was gory and excessive in its ferocity and she spent much of it with her eyes shut and trying to block out the sound. They walked back to the car, Emily deciding that she would now have to divulge her expedition which was fast approaching. A piece of fluff flew up her nose and she started a fit of sneezing which seemed never ending. Spluttering and half choking she rummaged in her handbag for a hanky to wipe her streaming eyes, found nothing so opened the glove compartment to see if she could find one there. She was searching around when her hand touched something hard. She pulled it out. It was a lipstick. She had never seen it before.

"Where has this come from?" she said. Seth looked over at what she was holding, saw the lipstick.

"It's yours, of course."

"No it isn't. I never use this make. Who left it there?"

"You haven't a clue what you have" he snapped. "You have a drawer full of lipsticks. I have no idea why you need so many. How on earth can you remember what you have when you have so many. What are you trying to say?" His voice grew louder and he was now shouting at her and the look on his face was such that she decided not to pursue the matter. She knew this was not her lipstick. It was far too fancy a make for her, one which she certainly could not afford. His aggression made her realise immediately that something was going on.

Suddenly everything clicked into place. The late nights working at the library with the so-called 'overtime' which never seemed to be reflected in his payslip. Was Anna the woman in question? He had never spoken much about her before inviting her to dinner. Could he really be so tactless as to have an affair and bring the woman into their home, together with the husband? He was so arrogant that she could believe it of him. Emily remembered how attentive he had been to Anna; the casual arm around the shoulder, the shared glances and seating her next to him so he could dance attendance on her. How could she have been so naïve? It now seemed so obvious she could not imagine how she had not seen it before.

Maybe she had subconsciously seen the signs but had buried them deep within her, unwilling to face the obvious and painful truth. Abuse is insidious, she realised. The victim is unable to understand what is happening until it is too late. It develops slowly, inexorably and all autonomy is lost. Emily realised she had been making excuses for Seth's behaviour from the day she had met him. The signs were all there but she had been totally blind to them. Her parents had suspected but had no proof, and Emily was so besotted by his charm that she had refused to face up to his faults. She now wondered also about his new antipathy towards Suzanne. What had caused that when he had always been so complimentary about her? Now she considered the idea that maybe he had made a pass at Suzanne and she had rebuffed him. Suzanne had said nothing on those lines but maybe she did not want to upset Emily. She would ask her when she went to London. The matter needed to be clarified in her mind once and for all. She was aware that Seth considered all women fair game and thought none could resist him when he turned on the charm. He might have made a move on Suzanne, she considered, because being such a close friend of Emily, the challenge of making her fall for him would be a huge notch on his walking stick.

She also appreciated that the ability for some independent thought still remained deep within her but she had to flee the scene as soon as she could otherwise be forever trapped in his clutches. There was no future in this relationship. Where did she want to be in ten years' time, she asked herself. The answer was a resounding 'out of this marriage'. She had to act and act fast.

In two days she would be travelling down to London. She now wondered if she should just stay down there with her parents. In other words, to abandon ship and leave Seth on Friday. Would there be repercussions and what would they be? Seth was arrogant and proud and had a strong sense of self-importance. Being deserted by his wife could easily tip him over the edge. She would have to give careful thought about how to proceed.

Emily sat quietly in the passenger seat so deep in thought that she was unaware of what was happening with the man behind the driving wheel. Suddenly she came to and heard him behaving yet again as if nothing had occurred. He was laughing and joking, asking if she had enjoyed the film.

"No, I did not. It was horrible. I hate all the violence that you seem to so enjoy. Why can we never go and see anything that I want to see? It's always what you want to see and I find that selfish and unreasonable," she heard herself say, being confrontational for the very first time in their marriage. Seth did not answer, just sat looking mutinous and angry.

"You always want to see those ridiculous love stories and sentimental rubbish. You can't expect me to watch that trash," he retorted.

"But you expect me to go and see the trash that you want to see with no thought of what I might like. In all our time together, we have never gone to see a film or play of my choice. Surely, we should accommodate each other occasionally. After all, marriage is supposed to be a partnership. It certainly is not in our case. I've had enough of this, and something has got to change." Emily heard her voice rising and knew that this was not the way to go. Seth would not listen to reason as he never considered he was wrong. One of his favourite sayings was, 'I'm not always right, but I'm never wrong'. That was a totally moronic and meaningless aphorism, but he thought he was so clever, and nobody ever pulled him up on it, including herself.

She realised that exactly was the trouble. She never challenged him on any of his bad behaviour. It had started so early in their relationship going right back to the time he had caused them to miss the train to visit her parents that long ago weekend. Why had she said nothing? Was she so pathetic even then that she could not confront his bad behaviour? What did this say about her as a person? Of course, by not standing up to him on the small matters this allowed him to proceed with his bullying and controlling conduct. This aspect of her personality dated back to her childhood, she realised, when her parents would insist that she had to abide by their rules and their standards. They truly loved her, she knew that, but there was a downside that rebounded on her in her adult life.

Even now, she consciously avoided challenging him about the lipstick, which was definitely not hers. She was frightened of him and of his reactions if she backed him into a corner. Her only way out was to get out from under and that was what she fully intended to do now. She had had enough of being a punchbag, both physical and metaphorical. This was the first time she had admitted to herself the extent of her fear and the strain she was living under. Constantly walking on eggshells, never fully opening up to him because of terror of how he would react.

The very first time he had hit her in the face, when she had told him she was unhappy about his behaviour towards Harriet, she had made the decision she would never confide her innermost thoughts to him ever again. This was a horrendous basis for a marriage.

Emily now made the decision that she would definitely not forewarn Seth that she was going to London. She would leave for the station straight after the school day ended and would leave him a note. Maybe this was cowardly on her part but it was also the sensible and safest way forward. She needed to protect herself. He could no longer employ his charm to ease her into acquiescence. That bird had truly flown, never to return.

Her pride was also her downfall. Had she not been so unwilling to speak out about the deterioration in her marriage to friends and family, maybe they would have made her see sense and act differently a long time ago. She was so ashamed and embarrassed by the situation and her complete lack of common sense in marrying this man. He had been her choice and hers alone. Blinded by his looks, his charm and outgoing personality she had not let his foibles and early petty behaviour intrude on her senses. She had shut her eyes to all the warning signals. They had been there in plain sight, totally ignored by her and now she was suffering the consequences. Her parents thought she was happy in her marriage. She had never given them the slightest inkling that all was not well in her world. Being so reticent and proud was her downfall and she dreaded coming clean to her parents. She just hoped they would support her in every way. Their wholehearted backing would certainly be imperative.

CHAPTER 20

They arrived home in silence. Seth parked their car in the driveway. She opened the door and went into the house. She decided she needed to keep her hands busy, so she went into the kitchen to put on the kettle. The concept of the panacea of a cup of tea solving all the problems in the English psyche made Emily smile drily to herself as she proceeded to make the universal cliché. It also gave her something to think about for a couple of minutes other than her marital problems.

"Do you want a cup?" she asked Seth as he came into the kitchen to put the car keys away in the pot they used just for them.

"I would rather know what you think you're playing about with this nonsense about the lipstick. Do you think I'm having an affair?"

"You tell me. I know for a fact that that is not my lipstick and you can shout and scream that it is, but no way is it mine. So how did it get into the glove compartment?"

"The trouble with you is that you're totally paranoid. You think everyone is out to get you, and you haven't got the sense you were born with." His voice was rising, making Emily back off to put a distance between the two of them, but the kitchen was small, and space was very limited. "No wonder I might be tempted to look elsewhere. You think you're so wonderful with your amazing family and an endless supply of money. And I'm supposed to be grateful every minute of every day. What do you know about real life? Everything to you is perfect and golden. You've never had to struggle in your life."

"So now the truth is out – finally. You're jealous. Jealous of my family, jealous of their comfortable life. Underneath all that charm and bombast is just a little man who tries to look big and important. Is that what makes you use me like a punchbag? Does it make you feel powerful and important?"

Emily saw his face go a deep shade of puce and then he was coming at her. She tried to duck under his arm, but he caught her on the shoulder, and she hit the floor with a crash. Then he was on to her, kicking her in the arms, on the shoulders and on her face. She heard the crunch of bone, and blood poured from her nose as his fist smashed into her face. She could taste the iron in her mouth and her eye started to close up. Then she felt his shoe in her stomach again and again. She tried to curl into a ball to protect her baby. What about her baby? What would happen to it? Surely it could not survive such a beating?

His arms pulled her up off the floor, but she fell onto her side, and he was banging her body on her side, down her shoulder and her hips. Blows rained down on her head, her arms, her face. It was never-ending. Her entire body was screaming at him to stop, to leave her alone, but she was helpless. Her hands went to her stomach, trying to prevent his shoes from thudding into her child. Her head was thumping against the floor, against her ear, and she realised he was going to kill her.

"My baby," she finally managed to scream, "my baby." Suddenly, he let her go. Her head hit the floor with a terrific crack. "What are you talking about? What baby?"

"I'm pregnant," she said, "and I think you just killed our child." She could hardly get the words to leave her mouth, which was swollen and hurting like hell. She doubled over suddenly, a fierce pain gripping her inside. She started to shake, crying and sobbing. "Get an ambulance," she managed to get the words out with barely a whisper.

He was white. The shock hit like a thunderclap.

"I'll take you," he stuttered and tried to grab her to get her on her feet.

"No, no, no" she screamed, "get an ambulance. They'll know what to do. I'm not getting in a car with you." She was sobbing, crouched on the floor in a foetal ball, clutching her belly and her entire being burning with pain and misery. No baby could survive this, she realised, and the hurt of the loss was like another huge blow. She could hardly get the words out as her mouth began to swell from a kick that had landed there. She could hardly breathe as the pain was so sharp and intense, which she knew meant broken ribs. Goodness knows what other damage there was. She could barely believe she was still alive, though she felt like the end had come. Her baby must be gone.

Emily heard him on the phone through a thick fog. She lay there on the cold tiles but felt nothing at all. Her mind seemed to be on another plane from her body, and it was as if she was watching herself from a high vantage point. She was shaking uncontrollably, piercing pains shooting through her stomach and through to her back. She felt like she had wet herself. What was that, she wondered but her mind could not get a grip. It was floating out of reach like it was on a cloud floating upwards and upwards, disappearing up to heaven. That would be a good place to be, she reflected. It would be quiet and safe with trees, birds and flowers, everything she loved.

She lay on the floor, waiting, tense, still. Seth stood as far away from her as he could possibly get. Something in her mind noted that, even now, there was no empathy, no apology. His face was white with shock at her revelation. She really did not care what he felt. All she wanted was for the ambulance to arrive and take her away from this house, this man. She never wanted to see either ever again. Who was this man whom she had chosen to marry? They had shared a home and a bed. He should love and care for her but his words of love were empty and false. He had used and abused her. He was a complete stranger, no part of her. She saw his handsome face and felt nothing but hatred and loathing. He repulsed her.

Time seemed to have stood still as they waited in silence. In fact, it was only a few minutes before the doorbell rang, and suddenly, the kitchen was full of large men carrying bags. Two paramedics went into professional mode, quickly kneeling down next to her and asking questions. The doorbell sounded again and two more even larger men in uniform filled the room to overflowing. They were the police who had been notified by the emergency call-out. The humiliation for Emily was now complete. Despite the pain and the shock, she was aware that she had hit rock bottom. How could her life have come to this, a beaten wife losing her baby on a kitchen floor, surrounded by men in uniform who were nothing to her? It was total humiliation.

She had to go to the hospital, they said and loaded her onto a stretcher, covered in a comforting blanket and strapped in place. She had never been in an ambulance before but she shut her eyes, glad to be out of that house. Seth had tried to get into the ambulance with her, but she managed to say 'no', and the paramedics told him he would have to come separately. She tried to blank out her mind, empty it of all thought and avoid what was happening to her. She knew from the sharp, vicious pains that her baby was going to be gone forever. She would never see him or her, not know what he looked like and what sort of personality he would develop. A lifetime of joy had been stolen from her. There would be no small person to lavish her love on, hold and nurture. So much had been snatched from her and could never be returned. And all this was at the behest of the man she had thought she loved and truly believed reciprocated her feelings.

The ambulance raced down the road to the nearest hospital, its siren blaring to clearing their path. Suddenly, she let out a piercing scream as an unendurable hot pain pierced her body, and she doubled up with the intensity of the cramping agony. The paramedic knelt by her side as she lost her baby. She knew it was gone, disappearing forever in a speeding vehicle through the streets of Manchester, and she hit a new, even greater, low. This was certainly the worst experience of her life, the most painful and the most degrading. She pulled the blanket over her face, unable to face the world and reality and quietly began to sob.

Arriving at the hospital, she was quickly wheeled into the casualty department and was surrounded by doctors and nurses. She heard one doctor call for an obstetrician. It's too late for that, was the thought that popped into her head. Hands were undressing her, vitals were taken as they asked so many questions of her. All she could say was, 'Call my parents. Please call my parents. Emily could hear a nurse saying furiously that they had to deal with too many women arriving in such a state. When would a stop be made to all this abuse? She was quiet now, totally numb, the tears finished for the time being. Now she just had to survive, and then she could grieve her loss, the child she would now never know. She had become a statistic.

Someone told her that her husband had arrived. "Keep him away from me. I don't want him anywhere near me. Please," she begged. The nurse nodded sympathetically and went off to send Seth packing. The time seemed to just disappear, and she was cleaned up, put into a hospital robe and taken to a ward. She would have to stay in for a few days while they assessed the damage and was safe from any consequences of the miscarriage. She was pleased with the respite this would give her, away from Seth and just waiting for her parents to come, comfort her and take her away from here forever.

CHAPTER 21

She slept fitfully. She had been given a sedative, which gave her some respite, but it was broken with nightmares of demons and images of violence and terror. She woke several times in a horrible sweat and convulsed in pain from all the bruising and damage. Two ribs were broken and a small bone in her cheek. Also her nose, which would need an operation to reset it. They would also have to do a D & C to clear out any remaining tissue in her womb. She had never been in a hospital in all her life, and now she needed two operations and goodness knows what other treatment because of the man she had married. She drifted off again.

Emily opened her eyes to a wondrous sight. Her parents were sitting on either side of the bed, her mother holding her hand and stroking it, a look of total misery on her tired face. They had driven through the night to be with her, shocked by the phone call from the hospital telling them what had transpired. They had not had a clue of what was going on, and it was difficult to absorb the knowledge of what their precious child had suffered for so long in silence. With their presence at her side, Emily finally felt safe for the first time in years. They would protect her, take charge and help her extricate herself from the tyranny which she had experienced for so long. She tried to speak, but it came out in a garbled babble through her swollen lips.

"Please, don't try to speak. There will be plenty of time to do that as soon as you get out of here and you come home to us," her mother said. Her father, who had been silent, now joined in

"I just don't understand why you told us nothing of what you were going through. Surely, you trusted us. I just can't comprehend this whole marriage thing. And now you've lost the baby," he said with such ineffable sadness. His face was lined and drawn, and Emily saw him ageing before her very eyes. She had suffered so terribly, but so were her family, and none of it should have been this way. She had been so scared of opening her mouth and telling the truth. But abuse and victimisation acted in this way, she now appreciated. She had been unable to see anything beyond her very narrow constraints to the world outside. She shut her eyes, overwhelmed by what had happened and by what she had done. Or rather, not done. The ripple effect could now be seen for the first time, which she had never envisaged. She had been so tied up in her own dreadful life she had not for a moment looked beyond. They were all paying the price of her silence.

"She needs to rest. Get her strength back and heal. We'll go and find a hotel for a few nights and come back shortly, and we'll bring some toiletries and other bits and pieces for you," her mother said, getting up from her chair. She leaned over Emily, smoothing back her hair and kissing her gently on the forehead. The touch of her mother's lips made Emily's eyes well up with emotion as she appreciated just how much she was loved and treasured, something she had sorely missed for a long time now.

A registrar came by to check on her. He had come to tell her that she would be taken down to the operating theatre for the D&C shortly. He explained what he was going to do and told her that, although she did not feel lucky at the moment, she was in fact, fortunate. He did not believe that she would have any problems having a child in the future so she was not to worry about that score. The thought had crossed Emily's mind, and that was now one less thing to worry about. Mind you, it still left many other huge issues to be dealt with, but this news was certainly a big burden off her mind.

The operation came and went. They had also operated on her broken nose, which had needed to be re-set. Back on the ward, she was left to her own thoughts. Her parents would return soon and she wanted some time to herself just to think about all that had happened. How had it all gone so wrong? Her mind flew backward in time to her early childhood, running through the long grass in the valley opposite her home in the scorching, brilliant sunshine. Trying to keep up with the other children and not wanting to get lost she saw again the magical flowers which glowed like jewels and so fired her imagination. Once again, she remembered that moment, gazing at the distant hills, when she had been overwhelmed by sadness. All these years later, she had never forgotten that instance of sheer melancholy. What had caused that? She had had no cause to feel unhappy. Life had been wonderful, full of love, beauty and joy. Was it a moment of premonition? Surely, she did not believe in such matters, but look what had transpired just a few years hence.

Seth had stolen so much from her. It was theft, pure and simple. Most people consider theft as taking something tangible, like a burglar or a pickpocket stealing from someone else. They are motivated by greed and making a quick buck without having to do any hard work. But theft can be something else altogether, Emily mused. There are people around who are totally oblivious to the needs of others. They feel no empathy and cannot relate to the emotions of others because they lack any depth of feeling themselves. This need to care for and to be cared for was totally lacking in Seth. This was theft of an entirely different hue. He had stolen her identity and her self-esteem. Gone, too were her individuality and persona. He had reduced her to a quivering wreck, unable to make a sensible assessment of her life. He had turned her into a victim. This was not just theft. It was grand larceny.

He had no concept of guilt and this he had demonstrated time after time. He would do something despicable and, within seconds had, completely put it behind him, not understanding the consequences and ramifications of his actions. Emily suddenly realised that she had married a sociopath. She had read about such people but had not appreciated that she was tied to one until now. This type of person is entirely selfish in his deeds and his actions, just desiring to give himself spurious pleasure, which would be entirely incomprehensible to her. He could not understand why she could not respond with love to his advances. He would abuse her and behave as though nothing had occurred, thinking she would immediately put behind her his obnoxious behaviour and it would have no long-term effects on their relationship. He could not join up the dots.

Emily considered his childhood and relationship with his parents. His father was not a pleasant man. That was a certainty, but he seemed positively harmless compared to his son. Maybe his parents appreciated the failings in their son and that was why the parent/child connection had been sundered. She would never know. Seth was a non-stop liar, and she would never be able to differentiate between when he was telling the truth and when he was lying. He had developed such skills in this regard, appearing outwardly charming and plausible while simultaneously plotting his next move to undermine and destroy. She had learned that about him the hard way. He said what you wanted to hear, promised the world, but made good on nothing.

He was clever. Emily granted him that but he used his brain for bad, not good. He would plan and connive while at the same time being a delightful company. He had the ability to split his personality into adjacent compartments. On one hand, he was charming and excellent company but simultaneously, he was scheming, sometimes for months, what he planned to destroy. It was an advanced form of hypocrisy in which the outer man soothed and persuaded at the same time as his inner persona conspired with his vicious deeds and words. He had stolen from Emily. His theft was not financial, although he certainly had benefited from her moneyed background. He came from a poor family and married her for her money. Emily could see that now, but that very affluence, which had granted him such a comfortable lifestyle, was also a source of envy and hatred to him. She had learned how he resented that he considered that he was on the receiving end of her bounty. All this was bad enough, but he had taken from her far more.

She gave it some careful thought. Finally, away from the marital home and also away from him, she had the luxury of thinking and understanding in a way she had not been able to while sharing a home and a bed. Her head was now filled with this whole new take on her marriage of which she had been wholly unaware. Her brain had closed down for the entire time of their life together. Suddenly, her mind cleared, and she saw Seth for what he really was. That was what domestic abuse does to you, she realised. The victims were the last to understand what was happening to them. She had lost her ability to think for herself and to be independent inside her own head. He had stolen from her her autonomy, forcing her to lose her total independence of mind and subsuming her identity. She had become an automaton serving his every whim and had morphed into an empty vessel unable to think or act for herself. It had become a submission. The illusion had dissipated and vanished into thin air. Seth had been in total control.

Lying in the hospital bed, she had the freedom to navigate in safety and without fear of the horror of the past few years. Now, she appreciated for the first time that she had closed her mind off throughout her marriage, never allowing herself to think or consider what was happening to her. No more; it was the time to extricate herself and rediscover her identity in a way that she had never before experienced. It would be away from Seth, no longer the willing attendant of him, of her parents even, however well motivated and loving. She would be her own person, independent of mind and action, controlled by no one and answerable only to herself. Yes, she would be considerate of others, empathetic and thoughtful, but at the end of the day would no longer be a victim of anyone else's perverted mindset. She would take care in choosing her associates in a way that she had been careless of in the past and would look beneath the veneer of charm to discover the person hiding underneath. There would be no more people like Seth in her life. That part of her was now going to be put firmly behind her. How to proceed would require careful attention but she would have the time to think cautiously of the future and her route through life. She had learned a salutary lesson, never to be repeated. This discovery had come the hard and painful way. That was a certainty.

All this thinking had exhausted her. Her body ached as she tried to find a comfortable position where her broken ribs let her breathe without agony. She shut her eyes and slept.

CHAPTER 22

"This whole business is so shocking that we're finding it almost impossible to comprehend," her mother said. She was opening packages from the nearest Marks & Spencer food hall. Salads and sandwiches were laid out on the side table, together with drinks and fresh fruit. "But we're going to have a long talk about how to proceed from here. The first thing is that we go to your house, pack a bag and take you back to London with us. You'll need time to recover physically and emotionally from all that has happened."

Her mother knew that she had been somewhat disconnected from her daughter when she was small. She truly loved Emily but had not been able to bond with her in the same way as she had done with Alex. Over the years, she had become more loving and warm to her daughter but now she wondered if their early association had somehow damaged Emily. Now, she was distraught to even consider that maybe Emily's reticence about the troubles in her marriage was partly a result of her behaviour years ago. This caused her severe anguish as she looked at her beloved child suffering so severely.

"There will also be the long-term consequences and how you want to proceed. You certainly can't go back to that house with that man," her father interjected. He poured his daughter a drink of fresh fruit juice and held it out to her. She didn't actually know if she would be able to get it down her though she was very thirsty and hungry, she suddenly realised. She raised the drink gingerly to her swollen mouth, grateful for the straw that had been provided. She looked longingly at the food. Her mother had bought all her favourites, which filled her with such emotion that it was difficult to hold back the tears. Her parents had so much love for her she now appreciated. Just the tiny gesture of her best-loved foodstuffs brought this home to her. She had forgotten what that felt like during her time with Seth.

"I'm never going back to him. That's over, totally done with. He killed my baby. I'll never get to meet him, and nor will you – your first grandchild. You have to help me. Seth will not let go easily. He liked the lifestyle I provided, the house, the car, which he had never had before, and he'll try and snatch as much as he possibly can."

"Don't worry about that, my darling," her father interrupted. "I know a really good divorce lawyer who will take him apart, especially with all this violence. You also haven't been married all that long, so that will play our way in the divorce settlement. You just concentrate on getting your strength back. I'll deal with the legalities. He might have conned you one way or another, but we now have his mindset, and he's more than met his match. He's a vicious bully, and bullies usually run for the hills when they are faced up to and confronted."

Emily nibbled at a smoked salmon sandwich, wincing as a scrap of crust touched the corner of her mouth. It hurt, but she was definitely going to give this food her best attention! She really was starving, unable to remember when she had last eaten. So much weight had been lifted off her shoulders with the presence and comfort of her parents supporting her. The physical pain would go. Losing her baby was such a deep hurt, and that loss would probably never fade. For now she would put that to one side and face up to it when her physical injuries had healed. It would not be overnight, but life would improve from now on. That she was sure of, definitely. She was already rediscovering her true identity.

She was to stay in the hospital for another couple of nights and then would be discharged into the care of her parents. The police were coming in the morning to take a statement about what had happened. They had come earlier, but she had been asleep after her operation, so the nurse had told them to come back the following day. Emily was in two minds about this upcoming interview. On the one hand, she wanted to tell someone in authority what had happened to her at the hands of this appalling human being. On the other hand, she also knew that the authorities were loath to interfere in 'domestics' and, most of the time would dismiss allegations of violence in the home as 'none of our business.' It would be interesting to see what would transpire and what the outcome would be. It was truly disgraceful that a man could beat his wife almost to a senseless pulp and just get rapped over the knuckles for it, yet a man punching another man in a drunken brawl in the street would be hauled off to face justice in the courts.

Whatever the outcome with the police, Seth's manic beating of her, which had led to this hospitalization, would play into her hands in the divorce courts. The police might do nothing and not charge her husband, but Seth had given her irrefutable cause for ending the marriage. Emily just wanted out of the situation, once and for all, with the minimum of aggravation so she could start the rest of her life. The hospital would provide a report of all her injuries, together with photographs, which would be the basis for her solicitor to demand a divorce and a settlement which favoured Emily. They would certainly apply for an injunction to keep him well away from her.

The three of them discussed their options. Emily most definitely did not want to see Seth at all. He almost killed her, and he certainly killed their baby. She could never forgive him for that. She did not think killing an unborn child was considered murder, but in her eyes, it most certainly was the case.

"You are staying in at least another night, so give us your key, and we'll go to the house and gather up as much stuff of yours as will fit in the car and take it back to London with us," her father said.

"If you go at around midday, he will be out at work so hopefully, you won't see him at all. He might make trouble for you. It's bad enough he abused me. I certainly don't want you to have to experience any of his nastiness. I'm pretty sure he will take my leaving him very badly and may become very hostile. He can be very possessive of what he thinks is his and I'm included in the list of his possessions. Please be very careful, won't you."

"It's certainly a thought. Surely he wouldn't try anything on with us? Maybe we should ask the police to come to the house with us. I'll have to give the matter some thought. He's not stupid, is he? He would be a complete idiot to confront us or be aggressive to us in any way. As I said earlier, he's a bully, and bullies hate to be confronted. In my experience, they only attack people they consider weaker than themselves and run when they themselves are threatened. They are essentially cowards. I think it will be okay," her father continued.

"I find it horrendous that we are even having this conversation. It breaks my heart that you have been put in this situation," her mother said tearfully. She wiped her eyes with a tissue, which she had reduced almost to shreds, as she twisted her hands in her lap. "I just wish you had spoken to us earlier and not let matters come to this stage. I feel so helpless now, and it hurts me to know how you've suffered all this time. How can any one human being be so evil? Never in my life would I have anticipated this situation and the necessity for this conversation."

Emily was starting, finally, to understand how her long silence and feelings of false pride had impacted the parents she loved. They may not have personally suffered the violence and abuse directly from her husband, but they were experiencing a profound sadness and feeling of helplessness, which was tearing them apart. Her guilt was overwhelming, and she felt her eyes welling up, and the tears began to fall. She was sobbing and shaking as the full horror of what had happened hit home like a sledgehammer.

All the pent-up misery and years of fear descended on her head like an avalanche of stones dislodged by a vicious storm. She doubled over in the bed as the sharp lances of pain from her broken ribs caused her to start hyperventilating. She was thrashing around in the bed, tangled in the sheets, screaming a torrent of meaningless, jumbled words. She was out of control, words and phrases overlapping inanely as hysteria overtook her whole body.

Her parents tried to hold her in their arms, but she struggled free, hitting out in a wild frenzy. !Quick, get a nurse," her mother screamed at her husband. At that moment, a nurse and a doctor rushed into the room to investigate all the shouting. A sedative was quickly administered. It took just a short time to take effect, and finally, Emily lay back in the bed, and sleep overtook her.

"It had to happen at some point," her father finally said. "Everything has finally caught up with her, and it's going to take a long time and a great deal of care to make her whole again. I wish I could deal with that nightmare of a man myself. I would happily swing for him. And I bet the police do nothing," he added bitterly. He and his wife sat quietly by the bedside, holding their daughter's hand while she slept. They had run out of words as they each considered the situation and the ramifications and fallout of a toxic marriage.

CHAPTER 23

"Well, that went as I expected. No surprises there," Emily's father said as he sat down in the driving seat and put the key in the ignition. Emily had been discharged from the hospital, and her parents had settled her down in the back seat of the car, propped up with pillows and covered in a blanket for extra comfort. The boot of the car had been filled to the brim with her possessions taken from the house so that Seth could not get rid of them, probably selling them to make some money.

"We knew the police would do nothing. Any man can beat up his wife with impunity, and there is no comeback. At least they put an injunction in force to keep Seth away from Emily. He can't come to the house or go anywhere near her. That's something, I suppose," his wife answered. "When we get home, we'll have to start legal proceedings and see what we can salvage from this whole disaster. In the meantime, let's just get on the road as quickly as possible."

Emily snuggled down in the back, shut her eyes and let the words just flow over her. She could not think straight at all. She was in agony with her broken ribs, and overall was the dull ache of her lost child. Legalities were the last thing on her mind. She knew her parents meant well, and she was very grateful, but at the moment, she was in no position to make decisions or life choices, so she was happy to let them take control. She was doped up with painkillers provided by the hospital and just prayed that she could get through this journey. She could not wait to put Manchester behind her and get back to her parent's home and the security of her old childhood bedroom.

No one had actually seen Seth. She had no idea where he was and presumed he was staying with a friend or found a bed-sit. She really didn't care as long she never had to interact with him ever again. Obviously, there would be matters to arrange. The house would have to be sold and a divorce organised, but for now, she just wanted peace and quiet and for all the pain to disappear. Emily had enough common sense to appreciate that there would be long-term consequences of the abuse she had suffered. It would affect how she thought, about how she behaved with other people, especially men. Would she need or want counselling? She had no idea. And how would she feel discussing her horror of a marriage with a third party? She was a very private person, keeping herself to herself, especially her emotions and feelings. She needed to do a great deal of thinking, but now was neither the time nor the place.

Her father pulled out of the parking space and soon came to the motorway and the road south. Manchester receded into the far distance as they headed towards London and home. No one talked much, and Emily managed to dose off for a while, lulled to sleep by the heavy-duty painkillers and the quiet hum of the car engine. Several hours later, her father turned into their driveway, and the long journey was over. A new page was beginning.

It seemed strange to be going back to her parents' home where she had grown up, been happy and innocent. How life had changed. Living in this house, she had never imagined what life would bring to bear. The cruelty and misery which had transpired were totally undreamt of. Even now, she could scarcely believe what had happened to her and how her life had panned out. Her brother Alex would not be in the house. He had actually outgrown his childhood persona and morphed into a very pleasant young man. He was now working for the UK Government attached to their embassy in Washington DC, carving out for himself a very successful career. It would be just herself and her parents in the house.

She walked slowly up the stairs and stood in the doorway of her bedroom, checking out the posters on the walls, the books on the shelves and her cheerful bedding. Nothing had changed in this room but it certainly had outside the parameters of this space. She was exhausted from the journey, certainly, but more from the events of the last few days and the years of build up to this moment. Her tiredness was overwhelming, not just lack of sleep but more a deep-seated lethargy, which was impossible to throw off. It felt like she was drowning. She crept onto the bed, curled into a foetal position and closed her eyes.

She woke with a jolt from a sleep full of violence, shouting and mayhem. Her eyes were gritty and she rubbed them hard, trying to rid herself of the imagery. Someone must have come into the room while she slept because the curtains had been drawn, and she was covered with a throw. She shut her eyes again and tried to motivate herself to get up, wash her face and make herself a hot drink, which she realised she desperately longed for. She would just give herself a few more minutes to compose herself before meeting her parents. They would have a lot of questions and she really did not know if she could deal with them at the moment.

Feeling at least superficially more human after washing her face, cleaning her teeth and putting on some clean clothes, she made her way down to the kitchen. Now a hot cup of tea was calling to her. Her mother smiled at her wanly and put on the kettle, took out mugs and placed a plate of mixed biscuits on the table in front of her daughter. Emily chose one of her favourites, a bourbon, and nibbled at it slowly.

"Did you have a good rest? I covered you with a throw but tried not to disturb you. You really need just to rest and get your head together," her mother said.

"I think I was totally shattered, and coming back to my old bedroom really took me to a new place, and I immediately flaked out. It's such a relief to finally be away from all that tension and nastiness. You don't realise while you're in the midst of it how much stress you're under, or even what you are experiencing. The abuse becomes normalised; just a part of your life and existence. Coming back here is helping put everything back into perspective and understand what a nightmare I was living."

"You should never have suffered this alone. If only you had given us even a hint of what was happening, matters would never have come to such a pass. I can't believe that a child of mine had to suffer such experiences and that you said absolutely nothing. You will now have to tell us the whole story. If nothing else, the divorce solicitor will need to know what has transpired and how that bastard treated you," her mother replied.

Just then, her husband joined them.

"I've unloaded the car and put your clothes, etcetera, in your bedroom and the rest of the stuff I've piled up in the spare bedroom. We'll go through it another time. There's no rush to deal with it all. We'll just take it easy today, and tomorrow, first thing, we'll begin sorting out matters regarding how to proceed. A divorce solicitor will be the first step. I have a good one in mind. Then we'll have to decide how to deal with the house. But the solicitor will guide us on that one. We'll deal with everything in good time. We just need to take our time and not rush into anything foolhardy."

"Seth will be furious that he has been thwarted," Emily interjected. "He'll do his best to get the better of me financially, and I think he will also do everything possible to stymie a divorce. He likes to be in total control, and he must be livid that I've now escaped his clutches and just walked away. I think he is very dangerous. You need to be careful. I wouldn't put anything past him. He definitely is a sociopath."

"There is an injunction against him. He'll be in trouble if he ignores that."

"That may be, but I don't think a piece of paper is going to worry him. He'll do what suits him, not the Law. He'll consider it a challenge, getting around that and pretending it doesn't exist. I know him. He'll be furious and need to get control back."

The three of them sat in silence, digesting this information. There was a lot to take in and consider. Emily's parents were only now starting to understand the mentality and mindset of their son-in-law. It was new territory for them and was completely out of their life experience. This is what their daughter had lived with and suffered. It was certainly far beyond their initial dubious considerations of him. What a hell it must have been!

The rest of the day passed quietly. Emily realised that she would have to let her friends in London know she was back home and why. She dreaded having to do this. She had left London with such high hopes, going to an exciting new life in a brand-new town. They had hugged and laughed, and she had been sent off with love. Now she was back, beaten and degraded both literally and metaphorically. In her mind, she decided not to let anyone know she was back until her bruises faded. They would have such pity and sorrow for her, but she could not face them, seeing the ghastly evidence from purple to black. She would phone

Suzanne, however. She needed her empathy and support, someone apart from her family to fight her corner without criticism or censure, just comfort and friendship.

Emily went into the hallway and dialled her friend's familiar number. Suzanne was so surprised to hear Emily's voice talking from London.

"Why didn't you tell me you were coming? This is such a surprise. I can't wait to see you," Suzanne exclaimed.

Emily was silent, not knowing how to proceed. Tears welled in her eyes at her friend's innocent joy. "Please come tomorrow. I need to see you badly. Everything is so awful, and I don't even know how I'm going to tell you what's been happening. Please just come," she finally blurted out.

"What's going on? What's happened? You must tell me. You're frightening me now."

"Tomorrow. I'll tell you tomorrow," she managed to gasp finally as she started to sob and slammed down the receiver. Emily knew that she must have really worried Suzanne, and she felt terrible about that but she just could not continue the conversation. She would have to deal with it tomorrow. Suzanne would have to know.

CHAPTER 24

Emily's mother gazed out of the kitchen window at the two friends sitting in garden chairs on the lawn. She would take them out some lunch soon, maybe sandwiches and a drink but was loath to disturb them. They had their heads close together and Suzanne had her arms wrapped around Emily. They had been out there now for more than two hours talking quietly though Suzanne seemed to be doing most of the listening. She had been horrified when Emily had let her in the front door. The sight of her friend's swollen, blackened face shocked her to the core of her being. She looked like she had been in a traffic accident or run over by a steamroller. It had never dawned on her for a moment that Seth was other than what he always seemed – charming and good company.

There had, of course, been that incident when he had grabbed her and tried to kiss her. She had shoved him away hard and made a joke about it, as had Seth. Now she looked back on that moment and realised that this was Seth showing his true colours. She had said nothing to Emily at the time but now considered that she could mention it, but not right now.

"I just don't understand why you said nothing from the very start. Why were you so secretive? It should never have come to this point. Please try and explain. I really am at a loss here. Even your parents knew nothing?"

"I was too proud and obstinate. I was ashamed and embarrassed. It's difficult to explain how abuse works. I've been trying to rationalise my behaviour over the last few days. It's just that when you are in the midst of it, you don't really comprehend what's happening. It starts off slowly and is so insidious. At first, you explain it away to yourself, and very quickly, you become a victim. Once you become that victim there is no way out. There is an undercurrent of fear – always – so you are scared to confront the person. I'm sorry. It's really hard to make someone outside understand what happens in a case of such cruelty."

"I became submissive and lost all my self-worth. Even my own identity disappeared into the ether. I can't tell you how angry I am at myself for letting this happen to me, how I seemed to become invisible and a nothing being. I've joined the legions of battered wives and am now just a statistic. And society doesn't help, does it? I'm so furious with myself to be in this situation. He has no morals whatsoever. He does what he wants, when he wants, and completely ignores rules and regulations. I was completely taken in by his charm, which turned out to be only a very thin, superficial veneer."

"You're right there about society not helping. How often do we hear rumours of 'difficult' men, but nothing is ever said, and it's all swept under the carpet? I can't believe about the attitude of the police. Big deal, they took out an injunction against him but will he keep to it? From what you've been telling me, that's a moot point. And divorce is still a big no-no, especially for the woman. She's considered tainted and somehow not fit for polite society. When is it going to change? I suppose it's not as bad as it was, but it certainly has room for improvement. I can start to understand why you kept quiet for so long. It really is appalling the way so many women get treated," Suzanne added.

The two young women sat back in their chairs to consider their conversation and its implications. Emily's mother chose this moment to bring out a tray of food and drinks, drew up another chair and joined them. It wasn't a very warm day, but pleasant enough, and it was good to be in the fresh air, which somehow seemed less polluted here out in the open, free from violence and the underbelly of life.

Suzanne left soon afterwards, and the family tried to lead as normal a life as possible, following the everyday routine of the household. Emily made an appointment to see the solicitor, Mr Mountjoy, the next day. He was a specialist in divorce law and his clientele included many high-profile people for whom he had achieved a very successful outcome. He did not come cheap but Emily's parents thought it well worth the outlay to achieve a rapid and beneficial conclusion.

The following morning, Emily drove with her parents to see Mr Mountjoy. She felt she needed their moral support, and they were happy to provide it. It would also be advantageous for them to ask questions that Emily might not consider or forget about. The solicitor's office was stylish and expensive as befitted his high charge-out rate but the man himself seemed very ordinary and easy to talk to, as well as professional. They were reassured by his manner and relaxed and let him take the lead. He asked many questions, filled a notebook with his writing, and carefully studied the photographs the hospital and the police had taken. He also spent much time going through the medical report, asking the odd question here and there for clarification.

They left his office feeling more upbeat and supported. As they did not know where Seth was staying, Mr Mountjoy said he would have the divorce papers served on him by hand, at the library. He had made discreet phone calls and ascertained that, indeed, Seth was still coming to work each day. The papers would be served the following day. No time was to be wasted.

They drove home, and Emily and her mother went into the house while her father went to see to some other business. Emily's bruises were still very fresh and evident, and she really did not want to face the world looking like she had just finished ten rounds in a boxing ring with a world champion and lost. Her ribs were also still very painful, and coughing or sneezing were agony.

She had told Suzanne that she could tell their mutual friends a little of what was going on. Emily really could not face telling and re-telling the sorry tale nor could she face the pity and horror she would see in their faces. It suited her to let Suzanne spread the word but she had told her to keep everyone away for the time being. Baby steps were the order of the day, she had decided.

Mr Mountjoy phoned to let them know that the divorce papers had been served on a very bemused and surprised

Seth. What did he think would happen when his wife had 'disappeared' from the hospital? Did he think he could just waltz back into her life as though nothing had happened, as he had done so often in the past? Emily had no idea where he was living and had no desire to find out. He was now part of a horrible past, and she wanted a completely legal, emotional and financial break from him. It was the solicitor's function to provide just that.

The days passed quietly. Emily's appearance was returning to normal even if her heart was still so sore from the loss of her baby. She hoped time would also heal that pain. There was no word from Seth and he had made no move to respond to the papers served upon him. This was unsurprising as this was now his only way of controlling and manipulating both Emily and the situation. Emily had closed the joint bank account and taken out all the money but made sure all the bills were being paid, including the mortgage. She did not want any problems on that score. All this extra spending by her would be taken into account in the divorce financial settlement, Mr Mountjoy informed her.

She was nervous, however, but kept silent so as not to worry her parents. Seth was too quiet. This was out of character. She knew he must be plotting his next move, and each time she left the house, she kept her eyes peeled for a sighting of him. She never left the house alone as it made her feel very vulnerable and exposed. Sometimes, when she was out with family or friends, the skin on the back of her neck would prickle with tension, and she would whirl around to check if she could see him. She never did. But that did not mean he wasn't there, just that he was being clever and she couldn't spot him. She knew well how devious he was.

She would gaze out of the window trying to see if she could see any suspect movements or strange cars. He did not have his own car but had shared hers, and her father had arranged for it to be taken to a lock-up garage until such time as they could drive up to Manchester to retrieve it. As the days passed she did start to relax her guard just a little and tried to persuade herself that he would not be such an idiot as to come after her in London, to her parents' house. As she had expected, there had been no reply to Mr Mountjoy, and the solicitor was planning his next move. It was not going to be a straightforward divorce, that was for sure.

As her face was not so livid in colour, she started to cover up her skin with make-up and dark glasses when she went out with her parents, still unwilling to venture out alone, knowing how angry and furious Seth would be at losing his 'possession' and his power. She had thwarted him, and this would not play kindly with his ego. She and her mother went to the shops together and walked around the park, taking time to sit and watch the world go by over a leisurely coffee and pastry, which felt wonderful after being cooped up indoors for so long. Her mother was delighted one day to see a smile on her daughter's face, fleeting as it was. It was a positive sign. Healing can be slow, both physically and mentally, but time and space should decidedly help, her mother considered.

Emily had still not met up with her other friends, but that evening Suzanne and her fiancé were coming to eat with them and shopping for ingredients for the menu needed to be purchased. It was a joy to walk round the shops, chatting about the choices available. There was so much pleasure to be gained from such a humdrum occupation, and she had not realised how much she had missed the sheer normality of such an activity. Stress levels in her marriage had been constantly at such a high level, and it was only now that she appreciated how bad her situation had actually been. Life could only improve from now on, Emily thought to herself as the weeks passed.

CHAPTER 25

The dinner with Suzanne and her fiancé had been a great success. Her friend had given up the endless round of dating, during which time she seemed to have gone out with most of the single young men in the London area. Now, she had found this delightful new partner. Although Emily had not joined in much of the conversation and banter she nevertheless felt more relaxed and took much pleasure watching the interaction between her parents and her friends. Suzanne's fiancé was a delight and obviously adored his wife-to-be, which made Emily a little envious of her friend's good fortune. He was called Simon and they had been an item for a couple of years now. He was a conventional guy with a steady job which paid well and a straight line of progression onwards and upwards. He was an excellent foil for the glamorous, outgoing Suzanne. Emily had not 'played the field' in the same way which had resulted in a lack of experience in judging personalities. This had definitely been an error on her part. Why had she not been more careful in her choice of partner? She had looked at the outside veneer but had not checked out the inside character. She would not make that mistake again but also realised that, although she had shown terrible taste in men, she was extremely fortunate to have such caring and supportive parents.

She woke the following morning feeling very lethargic after a restless night and decided to spend the morning in bed. Her mother came into her bedroom mid-morning to check on Emily and to tell her that she and her husband had some errands to run and also needed more items at the shops. Would Emily be all right on her own, she asked. They would be back before lunchtime.

Of course. I'll be fine. I'm going to be totally lazy and spend the morning right here. I'm feeling really pampered and spoiled," she joked.

"Good," her mother replied, "just stay in bed and don't answer the door. We will have the key and let ourselves back in, so you won't need to get up at all until you're ready."

The front door banged as they left, and she heard the car start up and leave. Emily gave a pleased sigh and turned over to make herself more comfortable as she snuggled under the blankets. She quickly dozed off. The house was totally silent while Emily continued to sleep on and off. For once, her rest lacked bad dreams and disturbing thoughts that had so blighted her nights recently. Added to this was that her physical injuries were finally healing, apart from the odd twinge from her recovering ribs, especially when she coughed and sneezed. The improvement in her physical health left her space and freedom to consider her options for the future. She had much to decide and consider but she was going to take her life forward slowly. There were going to be no more hasty or rash decisions.

She breathed contentedly, snug in her childhood bed and felt her eyes drooping once again, letting the mood overwhelm her and settled down to rest some more. There was no rush to get up; nothing forced her to climb up out of this cocoon of comfort.

Her eyes flew open. Something had forced itself into her subconscious, a noise perhaps? Was it in her head or in fact? She lay still, trying to listen if there were any sounds in the house. She heard nothing. Her imagination must be running riot. She tried to close her eyes, ignore the feeling and try to return to her sense of security of lying in her childhood bed. It didn't work. Something was nagging at her. Something was not right, an intimation in the back of her mind of a malign force somewhere on the periphery of her consciousness. Suddenly nervous and on edge, she rolled out of bed and put on the dressing gown lying on the chair, tied the belt around and went towards the door. Her hand was on the knob, about to turn it, when the door crashed open, hitting her in the face.

She let out a scream, and her hand flew to her face and came away wet with scarlet blood. She was pushed back and almost fell but just managed to right herself and stay on her feet as Seth barged into the room, almost falling from the impetus of his entry.

"Hello" he said in a conversational tone as he straightened up, as though they were meeting at a social occasion. "The door was locked, so I let myself in through the back. I smashed the window so your father will really need to get that repaired. I used a brick, very convenient, I must say, just lying there," he continued calmly.

Emily was almost catatonic with fear. His eyes were wide and without expression with a blankness that terrified her. His movements were like those of a zombie or a puppet, but with no one there pulling his strings. He had crossed a line from sanity to madness, she realised, which shocked her more than anything. She could see that he was no longer relating to the world around him and had entered a parallel universe. She had no idea how to handle this situation which was so outside her life experience. He certainly would not be open to a rational conversation. That was a certainty. There would be no arguing with him. He was way beyond that. There was no room to get past him as he blocked the entire doorway, leaving her no room to manoeuvre.

"You're coming with me" he continued in the same calm manner. "You're my wife. I own you. Did you think you could just walk away from me? You are my life, my love. You sent me legal papers. What was that about? Marriage. Let no man put asunder. Get dressed, and we'll go back home. Together."

"That's not going to happen," she said, trying to keep her voice level and not allow her panic to show. Suddenly, she was angry. How dare he break into this house, into her private sanctuary. "You have to leave. The police will arrest you. They took an injunction out against you coming anywhere near me. Please just leave. Now." She was screaming back at him furiously.

He started to laugh. It was even more scary than his calm announcement before. "I'm not arguing the toss. There's going to be no discussion. YOU. ARE. COMING. WITH. ME," he suddenly yelled, ditching the tranquil demeanour and lunged forward to grab her by the arm. She tried to dodge out of his reach, but he was quick as lightning and head-butted her. She felt the crack and a burst of intense pain as she screamed and fell to her knees. He was on to her, but suddenly, adrenaline and rage coursed through her entire body, and she managed to twist away and barge past into the hallway. Emily had had enough. How much abuse was one person supposed to tolerate? She was going to fight every inch of the way. He was no longer in charge of her. This was one fight he was definitely not going to win.

A split second later, he was coming back at her, and his foot lashed out at her, and she fell again onto the landing carpet. She wasn't having this, she decided. She had escaped him once, and she wasn't going to be his punchbag anymore. The thought brought herculean strength. She managed to twist away again and grabbed him by the knees, knocking him off balance. She fleetingly saw the shock on his face and the dawning realisation that he was, for the first time, not getting his own way. She scrambled to her feet, banging into him with the full force of her body, which sent him flying onto his back. She brought her foot down hard on his crotch giving her much satisfaction as he let out a scream of agony. Never in his life had anybody got the better of him and this provoked a reaction which generated a superhuman moment of force and ire. It was a battle which had been brewing for years. Neither was going to let the other win.

Emily headed for the top of the stairs, with Seth fast gaining on her. He caught her as she was about to run downstairs and rugby tackled her to the floor. He was going to kill her. She knew that now, but she wasn't going to let him. He was not going to have the last word in this disgusting marriage. She was now dangerously calm and composed. Never in her life had she hit another human being but now was definitely the time to start. She lashed out at him, catching him on the chin with her fist while she kicked him anywhere and everywhere she could. The two fell to the ground, intertwined in a bizarre mating ritual, each trying to dominate and win the game. Fists and feet whirled in a frenzy. Grunts and shouts filled the air. They were rolling, joined together in a seamless, moving marble sculpture. And then they were falling.

Falling headlong down the long flight of stairs, banging into the sides of the staircase, heads and limbs hitting the banister and the sharp treads, a grotesque tangle of intertwined body parts fused inextricably like some monster from the hidden deep. Neither made a sound as their descent continued to its inevitable conclusion. The end came rushing up to meet them, and the two bodies crashed onto the front hall floor with a whack of such finality as their limbs were stopped by the sturdy and unrelenting oak flooring. Then there was silence.

The two bodies, forced by the unyielding floor, had separated from their fusion at their final landing. Flung apart, one was resting by the foot of the stairs, its head twisted at an unnatural angle. The other had moved on, propelled by its own impulsion, to finish up near the front door. It lay still, a leg bent strangely backwards. Nothing moved. Total silence. The only sound was the ticking of the grandfather clock standing in the corner, watching sightlessly over them as it had done for decades. Tick tock. Nothing moved. The clock chimed the quarter hour. Tick tock. Then it chimed the half hour. Tick tock.

Relentlessly marking the seconds, the passing minutes. The clock's hammer started its noonday countdown with its pretty, gentle melody, so incongruous in this hallway of violence and then struck the harmonious notes. One, two, three. It continued, counting sweetly into the silence. Eleven, twelve. The final dong rang powerfully out across the otherwise silent hallway, demanding a response.

The body by the doorway seemed to understand, twitched and answered the call. One eye opened slowly, struggling to focus properly in the sudden glare and attempted to survey the scene. Then it shut again. Moments passed. Then, both eyes flew open and checked the scene again more carefully. They closed again.

A small smile crossed her face.

There is always a solution to every problem. You just have to find it.

Printed in Great Britain
by Amazon